"Nice Try, Sweetheart." His Low Chuckle Seemed To Vibrate Straight Through Her.

"I didn't say I would agree to anything. I said we'd talk."

She took a deep breath. "All right, cowboy. I'll stay with you at the Big Blue. But I want you to promise that you'll keep an open mind and give me a fair chance to change it."

"Only if you'll drop the matter if I decide against doing it," he said, extending his hand to shake on their deal.

The moment her palm touched his an exciting little shiver slid up her spine, and Felicity couldn't help but wonder what she had gotten herself into. Chance Lassiter was not only the best choice for redeeming his family in the eyes of the public, he was the only man in a very long time to remind her of the amazing differences between a man and a woman.

* * *

Lured by the Rich Rancher is a Dynasties: The Lassiters novel—A Wyoming legacy of love, lies and redemption!

* * *

If you're on Twitter,
tell us what you think of Harlequin Desire!
#harlequindesire

D1024099

Dear Reader,

When I was invited to participate in the Dynasties: The Lassiters series, I was thrilled to learn I would be working with some of my favorite authors and very good friends. We always have so much fun developing our characters and coordinating plots, and this time was no different.

In the fourth installment of the Lassiter family saga, *Lured by the Rich Rancher,* we see what happens when country meets city. Chance Lassiter, owner of the Big Blue Ranch, and Fee Sinclair, a public relations executive who works for his family's company, Lassiter Media, are as different as night and day. But when they meet at his sister's wedding, sparks fly and Wyoming nights have never been hotter.

I hope you enjoy reading Chance and Fee's story as much as I enjoyed writing it. There's nothing like a good cowboy story to warm your heart and put a smile on your face.

All the best,

Kathie DeNosky

LURED BY THE RICH RANCHER

KATHIE DeNOSKY

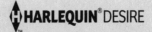

Special thanks and acknowledgment are given to Kathie DeNosky for her contribution to the Dynasties: The Lassiters miniseries.

Recycling programs
for this product may
not exist in your area.

ISBN-13: 978-0-373-73325-5

LURED BY THE RICH RANCHER

Printed in U.S.A.

www.Harlequin.com

Books by Kathie DeNosky

Harlequin Desire

In Bed with the Opposition #2126
Sex, Lies and the Southern Belle #2132
*His Marriage to Remember #2161
In the Rancher's Arms #2223
*A Baby Between Friends #2242
It Happened One Night #2270
*Your Ranch...Or Mine? #2299
Lured by the Rich Rancher #2312

Silhouette Desire

Cassie's Cowboy Daddy #1439
Cowboy Boss #1457
A Lawman in Her Stocking #1475
In Bed with the Enemy #1521
Lonetree Ranchers: Brant #1528
Lonetree Ranchers: Morgan #1540
Lonetree Ranchers: Colt #1551
Remembering One Wild Night #1559
Baby at His Convenience #1595
A Rare Sensation #1633
§Engagement Between Enemies #1700
§Reunion of Revenge #1707
§Betrothed for the Baby #1712
The Expectant Executive #1759
Mistress of Fortune #1789
§Bossman Billionaire #1957
§One Night, Two Babies #1966
§The Billionaire's Unexpected Heir #1972
Expecting the Rancher's Heir #2036

Silhouette Books

Home for the Holidays
   "New Year's Baby"

§The Illegitimate Heirs
*The Good, the Bad
   and the Texan

Other titles by this author
available in ebook format.

KATHIE DeNOSKY

lives in her native southern Illinois on the land her family settled in 1839. She writes highly sensual stories with a generous amount of humor. Her books have appeared on the *USA TODAY* bestseller list and received numerous awards, including two National Readers' Choice Awards. Kathie enjoys going to rodeos, traveling to research settings for her books and listening to country music. Readers may contact her by emailing kathie@kathiedenosky.com. They can also visit her website, www.kathiedenosky.com, or find her on Facebook.

This book is dedicated to the authors of Dynasties: The Lassiters. It's been a pleasure working with you and I hope to do so again in the near future.

And a special dedication to my good friend and partner in crime, Kristi Gold, whose sense of humor is as wicked as my own. Love you bunches, girlfriend!

One

At the designated time on the Fourth of July, Chance Lassiter and his half sister, Hannah Armstrong, approached the doorway to the massive great room in the Big Blue ranch house. "This seems wrong. I just learned two months ago that I have a sister and now I'm giving you away," he complained.

"That's true," she said, smiling. "But since you and Logan are good friends, I think we'll probably be seeing each other quite often."

"You can count on it." He gazed fondly at his five-year-old niece waiting to throw flower petals as she preceded them down the aisle. "I told Cassie I would come over and take her into Cheyenne for ice cream at least once a week. And I'm not letting her down."

"You're going to spoil her," Hannah teased good-naturedly.

Grinning, he shrugged. "I'm her favorite uncle. It's expected."

"You're her only uncle," Hannah shot back, laughing. "You have to be her favorite."

When he first discovered that he had a half sister from the extramarital affair his late father had some thirty years ago, Chance had experienced a variety of emotions. At first, he'd resented the fact that the man he had grown up believing to be a pillar of morality had cheated on Chance's mother. Then learning that Marlene Lassiter had known her husband had a daughter and hadn't told him had compounded Chance's disillusionment. His mother had been aware of how much he missed having a sibling and he felt deprived of the relationship they might have had growing up. But in the two months since meeting Hannah and his adorable niece, he had done his best to make up for lost time.

Chance tucked Hannah's hand in the crook of his arm. "Besides the standing ice-cream date, you know that all you or Cassie have to do is pick up the phone and I'll be there for you."

"You and your mother have been so good to us." Tears welled in Hannah's emerald eyes—eyes the same brilliant green as his own. "I don't know how to begin to thank you both for your love and acceptance. It means the world to me."

He shook his head. "There's no need to thank us. That's the beauty of family. We accept and love you and Cassie unconditionally—no matter how long it took us to find you."

As they started down the aisle between the chairs that had been set up for the wedding, Chance focused on the red-haired little girl ahead of them. Cassie's curls bounced as she skipped along and her exuberance for throwing flower petals from the small white basket she carried was cute as hell. Of course, like any proud uncle, he thought everything the kid did was nothing short of amazing. But with an arm like that there wasn't a doubt in his mind that she could play for a major league baseball team if she set her mind to it.

Approaching the groom standing beside the minister in front of the fireplace, Chance waited for his cue before he placed his sister's hand in Logan Whittaker's. He kissed Hannah's cheek, then gave his friend a meaningful smile as he took his place beside him to serve as the best man. "Take care of her and Cassie," he said, careful to keep his tone low. "If you don't, you know what will happen."

Grinning, Logan nodded. "You'll kick my ass."

"In a heartbeat," Chance promised.

"You don't have anything to worry about," Logan said, lifting Hannah's hand to kiss the back of it as they turned to face the minister.

When the bespectacled man of the cloth started to speak, Chance looked out at the wedding guests. Except for Dylan and Jenna, the entire Lassiter clan had turned out in force. But his cousin and his new bride's absence was understandable. Their own wedding had only taken place a little over a week ago and they were still on their honeymoon in Paris.

As Chance continued to survey the guests, he noticed that his cousin Angelica had chosen to sit at the back of the room, well away from the rest of the family. She was still upset about the terms of her father's will and refused to accept that J. D. Lassiter had left control of Lassiter Media to her former fiancé, Evan McCain. Chance didn't have a clue what his uncle had been thinking, but he trusted the man's judgment and knew there had to have been a good reason for what he'd done. Chance just wished Angelica could see things that way.

He shifted his attention back to the ceremony when the minister got to the actual vows and Logan turned to him with his hand out. Chance took from his jacket pocket the wedding ring his friend had given to him earlier and handed it to his soon-to-be brother-in-law. As he watched Logan slide the diamond-encrusted band onto Hannah's ring finger, Chance couldn't help but smile. He had no intention of going down that road himself, but he didn't mind watching others get married when he knew they were meant for each other. And he had yet to meet two people better suited to share their lives as husband and wife than Hannah and Logan.

"By the power vested in me by the great state of Wyoming, I pronounce you husband and wife," the minister said happily. "You may kiss the bride."

Chance waited until Logan kissed Hannah and they turned to start back down the aisle with his niece skipping along behind them before he offered his arm to the matron of honor. As they followed the happy couple toward the door, a blonde woman seated next to his cousin Sage and his fiancée, Colleen, caught his eye.

With hair the color of pale gold silk and a complexion that appeared to have been kissed by the sun, she was without question the most gorgeous female he'd ever had the privilege to lay eyes on. But when her vibrant blue gaze met his and her coral lips curved upward into a soft smile, he damn near stopped dead in his tracks. It felt as if someone had punched him square in the gut.

Chance had no idea who she was, but he had every intention of remedying that little detail as soon as possible.

Felicity Sinclair felt as if something shifted in the universe when she looked up to find the best man staring at her as he and the matron of honor followed the newly married couple back down the aisle. He was—in a word—perfect!

Dressed like the groom in a white Oxford cloth shirt, black sport coat, dark blue jeans and a wide-brimmed cowboy hat, the man was everything she had been looking for and more. He was tall, broad-shouldered and ruggedly handsome. But more than that, he carried himself with an air of confidence that instilled trust. She could only hope that he was related to the Lassiters so that she could use him in her PR campaign.

When he and the matron of honor continued on, Fee turned to the couple seated next to her. "Sage, would you happen to know the name of the best man?"

"That's my cousin Chance," Sage Lassiter said, smiling as they rose to their feet with the rest of the wedding guests. "He owns the majority of the Big Blue now."

Excited by the fact that the best man was indeed a member of the Lassiter family, Fee followed Sage and his fiancée, Colleen, out onto the flagstone terrace where the reception was to be held. She briefly wondered why she hadn't met him at the opening for the newest Lassiter Grill, but with her mind racing a mile a minute, she dismissed it. She was too focused on her ideas for the PR campaign. The Big Blue ranch would be the perfect backdrop for what she had in mind and there wasn't anything more down-to-earth and wholesome than a cowboy.

When her boss, Evan McCain, the new CEO of Lassiter Media, sent her to Cheyenne to take care of the publicity for the grand opening of the Lassiter Grill, she'd thought she would be back in Los Angeles within a couple of weeks. But she'd apparently done such a stellar job, her stay in Wyoming had been extended. Two days ago, she had received a phone call assigning her the task of putting together a public relations campaign to restore the Lassiter family image and Fee knew she had her work cut out for her. News of Angelica Lassiter's dissatisfaction with her late father's will and her recent association with notorious corporate raider Jack Reed had traveled like wildfire and tarnished the company's happy family image, and created no small amount of panic among some of the stockholders. But by the time she hung up the phone, Fee had already come up with several ideas that she was confident would turn things around and reinstate Lassiter Media as the solid enterprise it had always been. All she needed to pull it together was the right spokesperson in the right setting. And she'd just found both.

Of course, she would need to talk to Chance and get him to agree to appear in the television spots and print ads that she had planned. But she wasn't worried. She'd been told all of the Lassiters had a strong sense of family. Surely when she explained why she had been asked to extend her stay in Cheyenne and how important it was to restore the Lassiters' good name, Chance would be more than happy to help.

Finding a place at one of the round tables that had been set up on the beautifully terraced patio, Fee sat down and took her cell phone from her sequined clutch to enter some notes. There were so many good ideas coming to her that she didn't dare rely on her memory.

"Do you mind if I join you, dear?"

Fee looked up to find a pleasant-looking older woman with short brown hair standing next to her. "Please have a seat," she answered, smiling. "I'm Fee Sinclair."

"And I'm Marlene Lassiter," the woman introduced herself as she sat down in the chair beside Fee. "Are you a friend of the bride?"

Shaking her head, Fee smiled. "I'm a public relations executive from the Los Angeles office of Lassiter Media."

"I think I remember Dylan mentioning that someone from the L.A. office had been handling the publicity for the Lassiter Grill opening here in Cheyenne," Marlene said congenially. She paused for a moment, then lowering her voice added, "And when I talked to Sage yesterday, he said you were going to be working on something to smooth things over after Angelica's threats to contest J.D.'s will and her being seen with the likes of Jack Reed."

"Yes," Fee admitted, wondering how much the woman knew about the board of directors' concerns. Something told her Marlene Lassiter didn't miss much of what went on with the family. "I'll be putting together some television commercials and print ads to assure the public that Lassiter Media is still the solid, family-friendly company it's always been."

"Good," the woman said decisively. "We may have our little spats, but we love each other and we really are a pretty close family."

They both looked across the yard at the pretty dark-haired woman talking rather heatedly with Sage. It was apparent she wasn't the least bit happy.

"I know it's probably hard for a lot of people to believe right now, but Angelica really is a wonderful young woman and we all love her dearly," Marlene spoke up as they watched the woman walk away from her brother in an obvious huff. Turning to Fee, Marlene's hazel eyes were shadowed with sadness. "Angelica is still trying to come to terms with the death of her father, as well as being hurt and disillusioned by his will. That's a lot for anyone to have to deal with."

Compelled to comfort the older woman, Fee placed her hand on top of Marlene's where it rested on the table. "I'm sure it was a devastating blow to her. She worked so hard for the family business that many people just assumed she'd be running it someday."

"When J.D. started cutting back on his workload, Angelica knew he was grooming her to take over and we all believed she would be the one leading Lassiter Media into the future," Marlene agreed, nodding. "When he left her a paltry ten percent of the voting shares and named Evan McCain CEO, the girl was absolutely crushed."

Fee could tell that Marlene was deeply concerned for Angelica. "It's only been a few months since Mr. Lassiter's passing," she said gently. "Maybe in time Angelica will be able to deal with it all a little better."

"I hope so." Marlene shook her head. "There are times when even grown children have a hard time understanding the reasons their parents have for making the decisions they do. But we always try to do what's in our children's best interest."

It was apparent the woman's focus had shifted and she was referring to someone other than Angelica. Fee didn't have a clue who Marlene was talking about, but she got the distinct impression there might be more than one rift in the family.

"I don't have children, but I can imagine it's extremely difficult sometimes," she agreed. Deciding to lighten the mood, she pointed to the bride's table, where the wedding party would be seated. "I don't know who did the decorations for the reception, but everything is beautiful."

All of the tables were draped with pristine white linen tablecloths and had vases of red, white and blue roses for centerpieces. But the table where the newly married couple and their attendants would sit had been decorated with a garland made of baby's breath and clusters of red and blue rosebuds. It was in keeping with the holiday and utterly stunning.

"Thank you," Marlene said, smiling. "Hannah left the reception decorations up to me and I thought red, white and blue would be appropriate. After all, it is the Fourth of July." Marlene smiled. "We'll be having fireworks a bit later when it gets dark."

"Grandma Marlene, can I sit with you for dinner?" the adorable little red-haired flower girl asked, walking up between Fee and Marlene.

"Of course, Cassie," Marlene said, putting her arm around the child. "As long as your mother says it's okay."

"Momma said I could, but I had to ask you first," Cassie answered, nodding until her red curls bobbed up and down. She seemed to notice Fee for the first time. "I'm Cassie. I got a new daddy today."

"I saw that." Fee found the outgoing little girl completely charming. "That's very exciting, isn't it?"

Cassie smiled. "Yes, but Uncle Chance says that I'm still his best girl, even if Logan is my new daddy."

"I'm sure you are," Fee said, smiling back.

While the child walked around her grandmother's chair to sit on the other side of Marlene, Fee felt encouraged. She hadn't realized she had been talking to her new spokesman's mother and niece. Surely if Marlene knew about the public relations campaign and was all for it, her son would be, too. And with any luck, he would be more than willing to play a role in the publicity she had planned to help restore the Lassiters' reputation.

Seated next to his new brother-in-law at the head table, Chance was about as uncomfortable as an eligible bachelor at an old-maids convention. He didn't like being on display and that was exactly the way he felt. Every time he looked up from his plate, someone was either smiling at him, waving to him or just plain staring at him. It was enough to make the succulent prime rib on his plate taste about as appetizing as an old piece of boot leather.

Finally giving up, he sat back from the table and waited until he had to toast the bride and groom. Once he got that out of the way, as far as he was concerned, his duties as the best man would be over and he fully intended to relax and enjoy himself.

At least, Logan had decided they would wear sports coats and jeans instead of tuxedos or suits.

Hannah called Logan's choice of wedding clothes "casual chic." Chance just called it comfortable.

As he scanned the crowd, he looked for the little blonde that had caught his eye at the wedding. He hoped she hadn't skipped the reception. She was definitely someone he'd like to get to know.

He was almost positive she wasn't from the area. None of the women he knew looked or dressed like her. From her perfectly styled hair all the way down to her spike heels, she gave every indication of being a big-city girl, and he would bet every last penny he had that the red strapless dress she was wearing had a famous designer's name on the label. But it didn't matter that they came from two different worlds. He wasn't looking for anything permanent with anyone. All he wanted was for them to have a little summer fun while she was around.

When he finally spotted her, he barely suppressed a groan. She and his mother seemed to be deep in conversation and that couldn't be good. Since his mother had gotten a taste of what it was like to be a grandmother with Cassie, she had made several comments that she wouldn't mind him giving her another grandchild or two in the near future. Surely his mother wouldn't be talking him up as husband and father material.

He frowned. Of course, he couldn't be sure. She'd shocked the hell out of him a couple of months ago when she had admitted that she'd known all about the affair his late father had thirty years ago. Then his mother had surprised him further when she admitted that she was the one who paid child support to Hannah's mother all those years after his father's death. His mother's secrets had caused him no end of frustration and it had only been in the past few weeks they had started to repair the breach those issues had caused in their relationship. Surely she wouldn't run the risk of creating more problems between them.

Lost in thought, it took a moment for him to realize that Logan had said something to him. "What was that?"

"Time for your toast," Logan said, grinning. Lowering his voice, he added, "Unless you'd rather make us wait while you sit there and ogle the blonde seated next to Marlene."

"Did anyone ever tell you what a smartass you can be, Whittaker?" Chance grumbled as he took his champagne flute and rose to his feet.

He ignored his new brother-in-law's hearty laughter as he sincerely wished the couple a long and happy life together, then gifted them a thousand acres on the Big Blue ranch to build the new house he knew they had been planning. Now that the toast was out of the way and he had given them his gift, he was free to enjoy himself. And the first thing he intended to do was talk to the blonde.

Hell, he might even ask her to dance a slow one with him. Not that he was all that great at doing more than standing in one place and swaying in time to the music. He wasn't. But if the lady was willing to let him put his arms around her and sway with him, it would be worth the risk of looking like a fool.

Ten minutes later, after listening to several more toasts for the bride and groom, Chance breathed a sigh of relief as he headed over to the table where his mother, Cassie and the blonde sat. "I'm glad that's over," he said, smiling. "Now it's time for some fun."

"You did a fine job with the toast, son," his mother said, smiling back at him.

"Uncle Chance, would you dance with me?" Cassie asked as she jumped down from her chair and skipped over to him.

"You're my best girl. Who else would I dance with?" he teased, winking at the blonde as he picked Cassie up to sit on his forearm. "But we'll have to wait until the band starts. Will that be okay with you?"

Cassie nodded. "I hope they hurry. I'm going to pretend we're at the ball."

"Fee, this is my son, Chance," his mother introduced them. Her smile was just a little too smug as she rose to her feet. "While we wait for the dancing to begin, why don't you and I go inside the house to see if we can find your princess wand, Cassie?"

"Oh, yes, Grandma Marlene," Cassie agreed exuberantly. "I need my wand and my crown for the ball."

Chance set the little girl on her feet as the band started warming up. "I'll be waiting for you right here, princess." When his mother and niece started toward the house, he placed his hand on the back of one of the chairs at the table. "Mind if I join you, Fee?"

Her pretty smile caused an unexpected hitch in his breathing. "Not at all, Mr. Lassiter."

"Please, call me Chance." He smiled back as he lowered himself onto the chair his mother had vacated. "I don't think I've ever known anyone with the name Fee."

"It's actually short for Felicity." She brushed a wayward strand of her long blond hair from her smooth cheek as they watched Hannah and Logan dance for the first time as husband and wife. "My grandmother talked my mother into naming me that. It was her mother's name."

"Are you a friend of my sister?" he asked, wondering if she might be one of the teachers Hannah worked with in Denver.

"No, I'm a public relations executive with Lassiter Media," she answered as she picked up her cell phone from the table and tucked it into her purse. When she looked up, he didn't think he'd ever seen anyone with bluer eyes. "I work out of the Los Angeles office."

That explained why he'd never seen her before, as well as her polished career-girl look. But although she probably bought everything she wore from the shops on Rodeo Drive, Fee Sinclair had a softness about her that he found intriguing. Most of the career women he'd met were aloof and all business. But Fee looked approachable and as if she knew how to kick up her heels and have a good time when she decided to do so.

"I'll bet you worked on the publicity for the grand

opening of Lassiter Grill," he speculated, motioning for one of the waiters carrying a tray of filled champagne flutes. Asking the man to bring him a beer, Chance took one of the glasses of bubbling pink wine and handed it to Fee. "My cousin Dylan said he couldn't have been happier with the way you handled the opening."

"I didn't see you that evening," she commented.

He shook his head. "No, I had to be over in Laramie on business that day and didn't get back in time."

She seemed to eye him over the rim of her glass as she took a sip of the champagne. "I've also been put in charge of getting your family's image back on track what with all the controversy over J. D. Lassiter's will and Angelica's association with Jack Reed."

"So you'll be here for a few weeks?" he queried, hoping that was the case. "Will you be staying here at the ranch?"

"Lassiter Media has rented a house in Cheyenne, where they have employees from the L.A. office stay while they're in town on business," she said, shaking her head. "I'll be here at least until the end of the month."

Chance waited until the tuxedoed waiter brought him the beer he had requested and moved on before he commented. "I don't envy your job. Our reputation of being a solid family that got along well took a pretty big hit when Angelica pitched her little hissy fit right after my uncle's will was read. Do you know how you're going to go about straightening that out?"

"I have a few things in mind," she answered evasively.

Before he could ask what those ideas were, Cassie skipped up to them. "I'm ready to dance now, Uncle Chance. I have my wand and my crown."

"You sure do," he said, laughing as she tried to hang on to her pink plastic wand while she adjusted the tiara his mother had bought for her a few weeks ago. As if on cue, the band started playing a slower tune. Turning to Fee, he smiled. "I'm sorry, but I can't keep the princess waiting. I'll be right back."

Fortunately, all he had to do was stand in one place and hold Cassie's little hand as she pirouetted around him. The kid had definite ideas on the way a princess was supposed to dance and who was he to argue with her? He just hoped she didn't make herself too dizzy and end up falling flat on the floor.

When the dance was over and he and Cassie returned to the table, Chance held out his hand to Fee. "Would you like to dance, Ms. Sinclair?"

She glanced at her uncomfortable-looking high heels. "I…hadn't thought I would be dancing."

Laughing, he bent down to whisper close to her ear. "You witnessed the extent of my dancing skills with Cassie. I'm from the school of stand in one place and sway."

Her delightful laughter caused a warm feeling to spread throughout his chest. "I think that's about all I'll be able to do in these shoes anyway."

When she placed her soft hand in his and stood up to walk out onto the dance floor with him, it felt as if an electric current shot straight up his arm. He took a deep breath, wrapped his arms loosely around her and smiled down at her upturned face. At a little over six feet tall, he wasn't a giant by any means, but everything about her was petite and delicate. In fact, if she hadn't been wearing high heels, he could probably rest his chin on the top of her head.

"Chance, there's something I'd like to discuss with you," she said as they swayed back and forth.

"I'm all ears," he said, grinning.

"I'd like your help with my public relations campaign to improve the Lassiters' image," she answered.

He didn't have any idea what she thought he could do that would make a difference on that score, but he figured it wouldn't hurt to hear her out. Besides, he wanted to spend some time getting to know her better and although she might not be staying in Wyoming for an extended period of time, that didn't mean they couldn't have fun while she was here.

Before he could suggest that they meet for lunch the following day to talk over her ideas, she gave him a smile that sent another wave of heat flowing through him. He would agree to just about anything as long as she kept smiling at him that way.

"Sure. I'll do whatever I can to help you out," he said, drawing her a little closer. "What did you have in mind?"

"Oh, thank you so much," she said, surprising him with a big hug. "You're perfect for the job and I can't wait to get started."

He was pleased with himself for making her happy, even if he didn't know what she was talking about. "I don't know about being perfect for much of anything but taking care of a bunch of cattle, but I'll give it my best shot." As an afterthought, he asked, "What is it you want me to do?"

"You're going to be the family spokesman for the PR campaign that I'm planning," she said, beaming.

Because he was marveling at how beautiful she was, it took a moment for her words to register. He stopped swaying and stared down at her in disbelief. "You want me to do what?"

"I'm going to have you appear in all future advertising for Lassiter Media," she said, sounding extremely excited. "You'll be in the national television commercials, as well as…"

Fee kept on telling him all the things she had planned and how he figured into the picture. But Chance heard none of it and when the music ended, he automatically placed his hand at the small of her back and, in a daze, led her off the dance floor.

His revved up hormones had just caused him to agree to be the family spokesman without knowing what he was getting himself into. Un-freaking-believable.

Chance silently ran through every cuss word he'd ever heard, then started making up new ones. He might be a Lassiter, but he wasn't as refined as the rest of the family. Instead of riding a desk in some corporate office, he was on the back of a horse every day herding cattle under the wide Wyoming sky.

That's the way he liked it and the way he intended for things to stay. There was no way in hell he was going to be the family spokesman. And the sooner he could find a way to get that across to her, the better.

Two

The following day, Fee programed the GPS in her rented sports car to guide her to the restaurant where she would be meeting Chance for lunch. After their dance last night, he had insisted that they needed to talk more about his being the family spokesman and she had eagerly agreed. She was looking forward to getting her campaign started and his sister's wedding reception hadn't been the right time or place to discuss what she needed Chance to do.

When the GPS instructed her to turn north, Fee nervously looked around and realized she was heading in the same direction they'd driven the afternoon before on the way out of Cheyenne to the wedding. Sage and Colleen had invited her to accompany them to the Big Blue ranch for the wedding because she was alone in town and unfamiliar with the area. She'd been more than happy to accept the offer because her biggest concern when she'd learned that she would be spending more time in Wyoming was the fact that she was going to be completely out of her element. She had been born and raised in the San Fernando Valley and the closest she had ever been to a rural setting was her grandmother's pitiful attempt at a vegetable garden on the far side of her swimming pool in Sherman Oaks.

When the GPS indicated that her destination was only a few yards ahead, she breathed a sigh of relief that she wouldn't have to venture out of the city on her own. Turning into the gravel parking lot of a small bar and grill, she smiled when she parked next to a white pickup truck with Big Blue Ranch painted on the driver's door. Chance was leaning against the front fender with his arms folded across his wide chest and his booted feet crossed casually at the ankles.

Lord have mercy, the man looked good! If she'd thought he looked like a cowboy the night before in his white shirt, black sport jacket and black hat, it couldn't compare to the way he looked today. Wearing a blue chambray shirt, jeans and a wide-brimmed black cowboy hat, he was the perfect example of a man who made his living working the land. The type of man men could relate to and women would drool over.

"I hope I didn't keep you waiting long," she said

when he pushed away from the truck to come around the car and open her door.

"I've only been here a couple of minutes," he said, smiling as he offered his hand to help her out of the car.

Her breath caught. Chance Lassiter was extremely handsome at any time, but when he smiled he was downright devastating. She had noticed that about him the night before, but attributed her assessment to the excitement she'd felt at finding the perfect spokesman to represent his family. But now?

She frowned as she chided herself for her foolishness. Her only interest in the man or his looks was for the purpose of improving his family's image. Nothing more.

But when she placed her hand in his, a delightful tingling sensation zinged up her arm and Fee knew her reaction to his smile had nothing whatsoever to do with being anxious to start her ad campaign and everything to do with Chance's raw sexuality. He wasn't as refined as the men she knew in Los Angeles, but something told her that he was more of a man than any of them ever dreamed of being. She took a deep breath and ignored the realization. Her interest in him was strictly business and that's the way it was going to stay. Maybe if she reminded herself of that fact enough, she would remember it.

"I have some of the mock-ups of the print ads I'd like to run," she said, reaching for her electronic tablet in the backseat.

"Let's have lunch and talk before we get into any

of that," he said, guiding her toward the entrance to the restaurant.

"I suppose you're right," she agreed as they walked inside. "I'm just excited about starting this project."

His deep chuckle sent a warmth coursing throughout her body. "Your enthusiasm shows."

When they reached a booth at the back of the establishment, he asked, "Will this be all right? It's a little more private and we should be able to talk without interruption."

"It's fine," she answered, sliding onto the red vinyl seat. Looking around, Fee noticed that although the bar and grill was older and a little outdated, it was clean and very neat. "What's the special here?" she asked when Chance took his hat off and slid into the booth on the opposite side of the table.

"They have a hamburger that's better than any you've ever tasted," he said, grinning as he placed his hat on the bench seat beside him. "But I'm betting you would prefer the chef's salad like most women."

His smile and the sound of his deep baritone sent a shiver coursing through her. The man's voice alone would charm the birds out of the trees, but when he smiled, there wasn't a doubt in her mind that he could send the pulse racing on every female from one to one hundred.

Deciding to concentrate on the fact that he had correctly guessed her lunch choice, she frowned. For reasons she couldn't explain, she didn't like him thinking that she was predictable or anything like other women.

"What makes you think I'll be ordering the salad?" she asked.

"I just thought—"

"I can think for myself," she said, smiling to take the sting out of her words. "And for the record, yes, I do like salads. Just not all the time."

"My mistake," he said, smiling.

"Since it's your recommendation, I'll have the hamburger," she said decisively.

He raised one dark eyebrow. "Are you sure?" he asked, his smile widening. "I don't want you thinking I'm trying to influence your decision."

"Yes, I'm positive." She shrugged. "Unless you're afraid it won't live up to expectations."

He threw back his head and laughed. "You're really something, Felicity Sinclair. You would rather eat something you don't want than admit that I was right. Do you even eat meat?"

"Occasionally," she admitted. For the most part she lived on salads in L.A. But that was more a matter of convenience than anything else.

When the waitress came over to their booth, Chance gave the woman their order. "I can guarantee this will be the best hamburger you've ever had," he said confidently when the woman left to get their drinks.

Curiosity got the better of her. "What makes you say that?"

"They serve Big Blue beef here," he answered.

"It's the best in Wyoming, and several restaurants in Cheyenne buy from our distributor. In fact, my cousin Dylan and I made a deal when he decided to open a Lassiter Grill here to serve nothing but our beef in all of his restaurants."

"Really? It's that special?"

Chance nodded. "We raise free-range Black Angus cattle. No growth hormones, no supplements. Nothing but grass-fed, lean beef."

Fee didn't know a lot about the beef industry, except that free-range meat was supposed to be healthier for the consumer. But she did know something about Dylan Lassiter and the Lassiter Grill Group.

A premier chef, Dylan had started the chain with J.D.'s encouragement and had inherited full control of that part of the family business when J.D. died. Dylan was well-known for serving nothing but the finest steaks and prime rib in his restaurants, and Fee was certain that was why every one of them bore the coveted five-star rating from food critics and cuisine magazines. If he was confident enough to serve Big Blue beef exclusively in his restaurants, it had to be the best. And that gave her an idea.

"This is perfect," she said, her mind racing with the possibilities. "I'll have to give it a little more thought, but I'm sure we can use that for future Lassiter Grill advertisements, as well as the spots about the Lassiter family."

"Yeah, about that," Chance said slowly as he ran a hand through his short, light brown hair. "I don't think I'm right for what you have in mind for your ad campaign."

Her heart stalled. "Why do you say that?"

He shook his head. "I'm not a polished corporate type. I'm a rancher and more times than not I'm covered in dust or scraping something off my boots that most people consider extremely disgusting."

"That's why you're the perfect choice," she insisted.

"Because I've stepped in a pile of…barnyard atmosphere?" he asked, looking skeptical.

Laughing at his delicate phrasing, she shook her head. "No, not that." Now that she'd found her spokesman, she couldn't let him back out. She had to make Chance understand how important it was for him to represent the family and that no one else would do. "Not everyone can identify with a man in a suit. But you have that cowboy mystique that appeals to both men and women alike. You're someone who will resonate with all demographics and that's why they'll listen to the message we're trying to send."

"I know that's what you think and for all I know about this kind of thing, you might be right about me getting your message across to your target audience." He shook his head. "But I'm not real big on being put on display like some kind of trained monkey in a circus sideshow."

"It wouldn't be like that," she said earnestly. "All you'll have to do is pose for some still pictures for the print ads and film a few videos that can be used for television and the internet." She wasn't going to mention the few personal appearances that he might have to do from time to time or the billboard advertising that she had already reserved. Those were sure to be deal breakers, so she would have to spring those on him after she got a firm commitment.

When he sat back and folded his arms across his wide chest, she could tell he was about to dig in his heels and give her an outright refusal. "What can I do to get you to reconsider?" she asked out of desperation. "Surely we can work out something. You're the only man I want to do this."

A mischievous twinkle lit his brilliant green eyes. "The only man you want, huh?"

Her cheeks felt as if they were on fire. She was normally very clear and rarely said anything that could be misconstrued. "Y-you know what I meant."

He stared at her across the table for several long moments before a slow smile tugged at the corners of his mouth. "Come home with me."

"E-excuse me?" she stammered.

"I want you to come and stay at the Big Blue for a couple of weeks," he said, his tone sounding as if he was issuing a challenge. "You need to see how a working ranch is run and the things I have to do on a daily basis. Then we'll talk about how glamorous you think the cowboy way of life is and how convincing I would be as a spokesman."

"I didn't say it was glamorous," she protested.

"I think you referred to it as 'the cowboy mystique,'" he said, grinning. "Same thing."

"Is that the only way you'll agree to do my PR

campaign?" she asked, deciding that staying in the huge ranch house where the wedding had been held the night before wouldn't be an undue hardship.

The Lassiter home was beautiful and although a little rustic in decor, it was quite modern. If all she had to do to get him to agree to be part of the advertising was stay at the ranch for a week or so, she'd do it. She had a job promotion riding on the outcome of this project and she wasn't about to lose the opportunity.

"Nice try, sweetheart." His low chuckle seemed to vibrate straight through her. "I didn't say I would agree to anything if you came to the ranch. I said we'd talk."

Staring at him across the worn Formica table, Fee knew that she didn't have a lot of choices. She could either agree to go home with him and try to convince him to represent the Lassiters or start looking for another spokesman.

She took a deep breath. "All right, cowboy. I'll stay with you at the Big Blue. But only on one condition. You have to promise that you'll keep an open mind and give me a fair chance to change it."

"Only if you'll respect my decision and drop the matter if I choose not to do it," he said, extending his hand to shake on their deal.

"Then I would say we have an agreement," she said, extending her hand, as well.

The moment her palm touched his an exciting little shiver slid up her spine and Fee couldn't help but wonder what she had gotten herself into. Chance

Lassiter was not only the best choice for redeeming his family in the eyes of the public, he was the only man in a very long time to remind her of the amazing differences between a man and a woman.

Why that thought sent a feeling of anticipation coursing through her at the speed of light, she had no idea. She wasn't interested in being distracted by him or any other man. She had a job to do and a career to build and protect. As long as she kept things in perspective and focused on her goal of putting together a campaign that would redeem the Lassiters for any and all transgressions, she would be just fine.

The following morning, Fee had just put the finishing touches on preparing brunch when the doorbell rang, signaling her guest had arrived. "You have perfect timing," she said, opening the door to welcome Colleen Faulkner. "I just took the scones out of the oven."

"I'm glad you called and asked me over." Colleen smiled. "Sage is out of town for the day and I can definitely use a break from all of the wedding plans."

"Have you set a date yet?" Fee asked as she led the way down the hall to the kitchen.

"No." Seating herself at the table in the breakfast nook, Colleen paused a moment before she continued, "Sage is hoping if we wait a bit, things will settle down with Angelica."

Pouring them each a cup of coffee, Fee set the mugs on the polished surface and sat down on the opposite side of the small table. "When I saw her at the wedding the other night, I could tell she's still extremely frustrated with the situation. Has she given up the idea of contesting her father's will?" Fee asked gently.

She didn't want to pry, but it was no secret that Angelica Lassiter and the rest of the family were still at odds, nor was there any mystery why. The young woman wanted to break the will and regain control of Lassiter Media, while the rest of the family were reluctant to go against J.D.'s last wishes or bring into question the other terms of the will and what they had inherited.

"I don't think she's going to give up anytime soon," Colleen admitted, shaking her head. "Angelica is still questioning her father's motives and how much influence Evan McCain had in J.D.'s decision to take control of Lassiter Media away from her." Colleen gave Fee a pointed look. "But J.D. had his reasons and believe me, he knew what he was doing."

Fee had no doubt that Colleen knew why J. D. Lassiter had divided his estate the way he had—leaving his only daughter with practically no interest in Lassiter Media. Colleen had been his private nurse for some time before his death and she and J.D. had become good friends. He had apparently trusted Colleen implicitly, and with good reason. To Fee's knowledge, Colleen hadn't revealed what she knew about the matter to anyone.

"I just hope that I'm able to turn public opinion around on the matter," Fee said, dishing up the breakfast casserole and crisp bacon she had made for their brunch. "The Lassiters have for the most part been known as a fairly close, happy family and that image has taken its share of hits lately." She didn't want to mention that Sage had distanced himself from J.D. sometime before the older Lassiter died or that they had never really resolved the estrangement. It was none of her business, nor did it have anything to do with her ad campaign.

"The tabloids are having a field day with all this," Colleen agreed. They were silent for several long moments before she spoke again. "I'm a very private person and I'm not overly thrilled by the idea, but if you can use our wedding plans in some way to shift the focus away from whatever legal action Angelica is planning, I suppose it would be all right."

Taken by surprise at such a generous offer, Fee gave the pretty nurse a grateful smile. "Thank you, Colleen. But I know how intrusive that would be for you and Sage during a very special time in your lives."

"If it will help the Lassiters, I'll adjust," Colleen answered, looking sincere. "I love this family. They're very good people and they've welcomed me with open arms. I want to help them in any way I can."

Smiling, Fee nodded. "I can understand. But I think—at least I hope—I've found the perfect angle for my campaign and won't have to use your wedding."

"Really?" Colleen looked relieved. "May I ask what you're planning?"

As she explained some of her ideas for the videos and print ads featuring Chance as the family spokesman, Fee sighed. "But he's not overly happy about being in front of the camera. In fact, he's invited me to stay at the Big Blue for the next two weeks to prove to me that he's completely unsuitable."

Colleen grinned. "And I'm assuming you're going to use that time to convince him the exact opposite is true."

"Absolutely," Fee said, laughing. "He has no idea how persistent I can be when I know I'm right."

"Well, I wish you the best of luck with that," Colleen said, reaching for a scone. "I've heard Sage mention how stubborn Chance could be when they were kids."

Fee grinned. "Then I'd say he's met his match because once I've made up my mind I don't give up."

"The next couple of weeks should be very interesting on the Big Blue ranch," Colleen said, laughing. "What I wouldn't give to be a fly on the wall when the two of you butt heads."

"I'm not only hoping to have his agreement within a week, I'd like to get a photographer to start taking still shots for the first print ads," Fee confided in her new friend. "Most of those will start running by the end of the month."

"It sounds like you have things under control." Colleen took a sip of her coffee. "I'll keep my fingers crossed that you get Chance to go along with all of it."

"Thanks," Fee said, nibbling on her scone.

She didn't tell Colleen, but she had to get him on board. Her entire campaign was based on him and his down-to-earth cowboy persona. The Lassiter family had been ranching in Wyoming for years before Lassiter Media became the communications giant it was today. Besides the down-to-earth appeal of a cowboy, it just made sense to capitalize on the family's Western roots. She wasn't going to let a little thing like Chance's reluctance to be in front of the camera deter her from what she knew would be an outstanding promotion.

On Monday afternoon when Chance parked his truck in front of the house Lassiter Media had rented for visiting executives, he felt a little guilty about the deal he had made with Fee. He had promised that he would consider her arguments for his being part of her PR campaign and he did intend to think about it.

It wasn't that he didn't want to help the family; he just couldn't see why one of his cousins wasn't more suitable for the job of spokesman or for that matter, even his mother. She was the family matriarch and had been since his aunt Ellie had died over twenty-eight years ago. They all knew more about Lassiter Media than he did. He was a rancher and had been all of his life. That's the way he liked it and wanted it to stay. Besides, he'd never been the type who felt the need to draw a lot of attention to himself. He had always been comfortable with who he was and hadn't seen any reason to seek out the approval of people whose opinions of him didn't matter.

All he wanted was to get to know Fee better and that was the main reason he'd suggested that she stay with him on the ranch. They could have some fun together and at the same time, he could prove to her that he wasn't the man she needed for her ad campaign. He knew she wasn't going to give up easily and would probably still insist that he was the best choice. But he seriously doubted she was going to make a lot of headway with her efforts.

Getting out of the truck, he walked up to the front door and raised his hand to ring the bell just as Fee opened it. "Are you ready to go?" he asked as his gaze wandered from her head to her toes.

Dressed in khaki slacks and a mint-green blouse, she'd styled her long blond hair in loose curls, making her look more as if she was ready for a day of shopping in some chic, high-end boutique than going to stay at a working cattle ranch. He hadn't thought it was possible for the woman to be any prettier than she had been two days ago when they'd had lunch, but she'd proved him wrong.

"I think I'm about as ready as I'll ever be," she said, pulling a bright pink suitcase behind her as she stepped out onto the porch.

His eyebrows rose when he glanced down at the luggage. It was big enough to fit a body and if the bulging sides were any indication, there just might be one in there already. It was completely stuffed and he couldn't imagine what all she had in it.

"Think you have enough clothes to last you for two weeks?" he asked, laughing.

"I wasn't sure what I would need," she answered, shrugging one slender shoulder. "Other than attending the wedding the other night, I've never been on a ranch before."

"My place does have the convenience of a washer and dryer," he quipped.

"I thought it would," she said, giving him one of those long-suffering looks women give men they think are a little simpleminded. "That's why I packed light."

When he picked up the suitcase, he frowned. The damn thing weighed at least as much as a tightly packed bale of hay. If this was her idea of "packing light," he couldn't imagine how many pieces of luggage she'd brought with her for her stay in Cheyenne.

Placing his other hand at the small of her back, he noticed she was wearing a pair of strappy sandals as he guided her out to his truck. "I'm betting you don't have a pair of boots packed in here," he said, opening the rear door on the passenger side of the club cab to stow the suitcase.

"No. I didn't expect to be needing them," she answered. She paused a moment before she asked, "What would I need them for?"

He laughed. "Oh, just a couple of things like walking and riding."

"I…I'm going to be riding?" she asked, sounding a little unsure. "A…horse?"

"Yup." He closed the rear door, then turned to help her into the front passenger seat. "Unless you want me to saddle up a steer so you can give that a try."

She vigorously shook her head. "No."

"You do know how to ride, don't you?"

There was doubt in her pretty blue eyes when she looked at him and he knew the answer before she opened her mouth. "The closest I've ever been to a horse is seeing them in parades."

"Don't worry. It's pretty easy. I'll teach you," he said, giving her what he hoped was an encouraging smile as he placed his hands around her waist.

"W-what are you doing?" she asked, placing her hands on his chest. The feel of her warm palms seemed to burn right through the fabric and had him wondering how they would feel on his bare chest.

"You're short and…the truck is pretty tall," he said, trying to ignore the hitch he'd suddenly developed in his breathing. "I thought I'd help you out."

"I assure you, I could climb into the truck," she said.

"I'm sure you could," he said, smiling. "But you want to shoot me a break here? I'm trying to be a gentleman."

Staring down at her, it was all he could do to keep from covering her lips with his and kissing her until the entire neighborhood was thoroughly scandalized. His heart stuttered when he realized she looked as if she wanted him to do just that.

He wasn't sure how long they continued to gaze at each other, but when he finally had the presence of mind to lift her onto the seat, he quickly closed the truck door and walked around to climb in behind the steering wheel. What the hell was wrong with him? he wondered as he started the engine and steered away from the curb. He'd never before been so completely mesmerized by a woman that he forgot what he was doing. Why was Fee different? What was it about her that made him act like an inexperienced teenager on his first date?

"I still don't understand…why you insisted on coming to get me," she said, sounding delightfully breathless. "I could have driven…to the ranch."

"You could have tried," he said, focusing on her statement instead of her perfect coral lips. "But that low-slung little sports car wouldn't have made it without drowning out when you forded the creek. That's why I suggested you leave it here. If you need to go somewhere, I'll be more than happy to take you."

"When we drove to the ranch for the wedding, I don't remember anywhere along the way that could happen," she said as if she didn't believe him. "The roads were all asphalt and so was the lane leading up to the ranch house." She frowned. "I don't even remember a bridge."

"There isn't one," he answered. "Most of the year it's just a little slow-moving stream about three or four inches deep and about two feet wide," he explained. "But July is the wettest month we have here in Wyoming. It rains almost every day and the stream doubles in size and depth. That little car sits so low it would stall out in a heartbeat."

"Why don't you build a bridge?" she demanded. "It seems to me it would be more convenient than running the risk of a vehicle stalling out."

He nodded. "Eventually I'll have the road to my place asphalted and a culvert or bridge put in. But I only inherited the ranch a few months ago and I've had other things on my mind like cutting and baling hay, mending fences and moving cattle from one pasture to another."

"Hold it just a minute. Your place?" She frowned. "You don't live on the Big Blue ranch?"

"I've never lived anywhere else," he admitted. "I just don't live in the main house."

"There's another house on the ranch?" she asked, her tone doubtful.

"Actually there are several," he said, nodding. "There's the main house, the Lassiter homestead where I live, as well as a foreman's cottage and a couple of smaller houses for married hired hands."

"The only buildings I saw close to the ranch house were a couple of barns, a guest cottage and a stable," she said, sounding skeptical.

"You can't see the other places from the main house," he answered. "Those are about five miles down the road where I live."

"So I won't be staying with Marlene?" she inquired, as if she might be rethinking her decision to stay with him.

"Nope. The actual ranch headquarters is where we'll be staying," he said, wondering if Fee was apprehensive about being alone with him. She needn't be. He might want to get to know her on a very personal level, but he wasn't a man who forced his attentions on a woman if she didn't want them.

Frowning, she nibbled on her lower lip as if deep in thought. "I was led to believe that the main house was the ranch headquarters."

Chance almost groaned aloud. Nothing would please him more than to cover her mouth with his and do a little nibbling of his own. Fortunately, he didn't have time to dwell on it. They had arrived at the stop he'd decided to make when he learned she didn't have a pair of boots.

Steering his truck into the parking lot at the Wild Horse Western Wear store on the northern outskirts of Cheyenne, he parked and turned to face her. "My uncle built the main house when he and my late aunt adopted Sage and Dylan. That's where we have our family gatherings, entertain guests, and Lassiter Media holds corporate receptions. The actual ranch headquarters has always been at the home my grandfather and grandmother built when they first came to Wyoming. I renovated it about seven years back when my uncle turned the running of the ranch over to me. I've lived there ever since."

She looked confused. "Why not have the headquarters at the main house? Doesn't that make more sense?"

Laughing, he shook his head. "Headquarters is

where we sort cattle for taking them to market and quarantine and treat sick livestock. A herd of cattle can be noisy and churn up a lot of dust when it's dry. That's not something you want guests to have to contend with when you're throwing a party or trying to make a deal with business associates."

"I suppose that makes sense," she finally said, as if she was giving it some serious thought.

"Now that we have that settled, let's go get you fitted for a pair of boots," he suggested, getting out of the truck and walking around to help her down from the passenger seat. "How many pairs of jeans did you bring?"

"Two," she said as they walked into the store. "Why?"

"I'm betting your jeans have some designer dude's name on the hip pocket and cost a small fortune," he explained as he walked her over to the women's section.

"As a matter of fact, I did get them from a boutique on Rodeo Drive," she said, frowning. "Does that make them unsuitable?"

"That depends," he answered truthfully. "If you don't mind running the risk of getting them torn or stained up, they'll be just fine. But if they're very expensive, I doubt you'll want to do that. Besides, they probably aren't boot cut, are they?"

"No. They're skinny jeans."

He swallowed hard as he imagined what she would look like in the form-fitting pants. "We'll pick up a few pairs of jeans and a hat."

"I don't wear hats," she said, her long blond hair swaying as she shook her head.

Without thinking, Chance reached up to run his index finger along her smooth cheek. "I'd hate to see your pretty skin damaged by the sun. You'll need a hat to protect against sun and windburn."

As she stared up at him, her pink tongue darted out to moisten her lips and it was all he could do to keep from taking her into his arms to find out if they tasted as sweet as they looked. Deciding there would be plenty of time in the next two weeks to find out, he forced himself to move. He suddenly couldn't wait to get to the ranch.

"Let's get you squared away with jeans and boots," he advised. "Then we'll worry about that hat."

Three

Fee glanced down at her new jeans, boots and hot-pink T-shirt with *I love Wyoming* screen-printed on the front as Chance drove away from the store. When had she lost control of the situation? When they walked into the store, she hadn't intended to get anything but a pair of boots and maybe a couple pairs of jeans.

She had to admit that Chance had been right about her needing the boots. Her sandals definitely weren't the right choice of footwear if she was going to be around large animals. Even his suggestion about getting new jeans had made sense. She'd paid far too much for the stylish denim she'd purchased in one of the boutiques on Rodeo Drive to ruin them.

But when he had suggested that she might want

to start wearing the boots right away to get them broken in, that's when her command of the situation went downhill in a hurry. She'd had to put on a pair of the new jeans because the legs of her khaki slacks hadn't fit over the tops of the boots. Then she'd taken one look at her raw silk blouse with the new jeans and boots and decided to get something more casual, motivating her to get the T-shirt. She glanced at the hat sitting beside her on the truck seat. She'd even given in to getting the hat because his argument about protecting her skin had made sense.

Looking over at Chance, she had to admit that a shopping trip had never been as exhilarating as it had been with him. When she stepped out of the dressing room to check in the full-length mirror how her new jeans and T-shirt fit, she'd seen an appreciation in his brilliant green eyes that thrilled her all the way to her toes. It certainly beat the practiced comments of a boutique employee just wanting to make a sale.

She sighed heavily. Now that they were actually on the road leading to the ranch, she couldn't help but wonder what she'd gotten herself into. On some level, she had been excited about the new experience of being on a working ranch. It was something she'd never done before and although she felt as if she would be going into the great unknown, she had thought she was ready for the challenge. But if the past hour and a half was any indication of how far out of her element she was, she couldn't imagine what the next two weeks held for her.

Preoccupied with her new clothes and how ill-prepared she had been for her stay at the ranch, it came as no small surprise when Chance drove past the lane leading up to the main house on the Big Blue ranch. They had traveled the thirty or so miles without her even realizing it.

Now as she watched the lane disappear behind them in the truck's side mirror, Fee felt the butterflies begin to gather in her stomach. It was as if they were leaving civilization behind and embarking on a journey into the untamed wilderness.

She was a born and bred city dweller and the closest she had ever been to any kind of predatory wildlife was in the confines of a zoo. There was a certain comfort in knowing that there were iron bars and thick plates of glass between her and the creatures that would like nothing more than to make a meal out of her. But out in the wilds of Wyoming those safety measures were nonexistent and she knew as surely as she knew her own name there were very large, very hairy animals with long claws and big teeth hiding behind every bush and tree, just waiting for the opportunity to pounce on her.

"Do you have a lot of trouble with predators?" she asked when the asphalt road turned into a narrow gravel lane.

Chance shrugged. "Once in a while we have a mountain lion or bobcat wander down from the higher elevations, but most of the time the only wildlife we see are antelope and deer."

"Doesn't Wyoming have bears and wolves?" she asked, remembering something she'd read about their being a problem when she'd gone online the night before to research ranching in Wyoming.

"Yeah, but they're like the big cats. They usually stay up in the mountains where their food sources are," he said slowly. "Why?"

"I just wondered," she said, looking out the passenger window.

She didn't like being afraid. It took control away from her and made her feel inadequate. Fee couldn't think of anything that she hated more than not being in charge of herself. But that was exactly the way she was feeling at the moment. But as long as the really big, extremely scary wildlife stayed in the mountains where they belonged, she'd be just fine.

As she stared at the vast landscape, hundreds of black dots came into view. As they got closer, she realized the dots were cattle. "Are all those yours?"

"Yup. That's some of them."

"How big is this ranch?" she asked, knowing they had been on the property for several miles.

"We have thirty thousand acres," Chance answered proudly. "My grandparents settled here when they first got married. Then when Uncle J.D. inherited it, he kept buying up land until it grew to the size it is now." He laughed. "And believe it or not, I'm going to be checking into leasing another ten or twenty thousand acres from the Bureau of Land Management next year."

"Isn't the ranch big enough for you?" she asked before she could stop herself. It seemed to her that much land should be more than enough for anyone.

"Not really." He smiled as he went on to explain. "The Big Blue has around six thousand head of cattle at any given time. Since our cattle are grass-fed year-round we have to be careful to manage the pastures to keep from overgrazing, as well as make sure we have enough graze to mow for hay in the summer to put up for the winter months. That's why we keep a constant check on grazing conditions and move the herds frequently. Having the extra land would give us some breathing room with that, as well as expanding the herd."

His knowledge about the needs of the cattle he raised impressed her and Fee made a mental note of the information. Since he supplied beef for the Lassiter Grill Group, it was definitely something she could envision using if she was assigned future promotions for the restaurant chain.

When Chance stopped the truck on top of a ridge, Fee's breath caught at the sight of the valley below. It looked like a scene out of a Western movie. "This is where you live?"

Smiling proudly, he nodded. "This is the Lassiter homestead. The house wasn't always this big, though. When I did the renovations before I moved in, I added several rooms and the wraparound porch on to the original log cabin."

"It's really beautiful," Fee said, meaning it. She pointed to two small houses on the far side of the valley. "Are those the cottages you mentioned for the married hired hands?"

"Slim and Lena Garrison live in one and Hal and

June Wilson live in the other," Chance answered. "Slim is the ranch foreman and Hal is the head wrangler." He pointed toward a good-size log structure not far from the three barns behind the house. "That's the bunkhouse, where the single guys stay."

"This would be the perfect place to film some of the videos I'm planning," Fee said, thinking aloud. She noticed that Chance didn't comment as he restarted the truck and drove down into the valley. "You do realize that I'm not going to give up until you agree to be the Lassiter spokesman, don't you?"

"It never crossed my mind that you would," he said, grinning as he parked the truck in front of the house. He got out to come around and open her door. "You're here to try to talk me into taking on the job and I'm going to try to convince you that you'd be better off finding someone else."

Anything she was about to say lodged in her throat when he lifted her from the truck and set her on her feet. She placed her hands on his biceps to steady herself and the latent strength she felt beneath his chambray shirt caused her pulse to race and an interesting little flutter in a part of her that had no business fluttering.

"Why do you keep…doing that?" she asked.

"What?"

"You keep lifting me in and out of the truck," she said, even though she enjoyed the feel of his solid strength beneath her palms. "I'm perfectly capable of doing that for myself."

"Two reasons, sweetheart." He leaned close to

whisper, "I'm trying to be helpful. But more than that, I like touching you."

Her breath caught and when her gaze locked with his, she wasn't sure if she would ever breathe again. He was going to kiss her. And heaven help her, she was going to let him.

But instead of lowering his head to capture her lips with his, Chance took a deep breath a moment before he stepped back and turned to get her luggage from the backseat. She did her best to cover her disappointment by looking beyond the house toward the fenced-in areas around the barn.

"What are all these pens used for?" she asked.

"We use the bigger ones for sorting the herds during roundup," he answered as he closed the truck door. "The smaller ones are for sick or injured animals that need to be treated or quarantined. The round one we use for training the working stock or breaking them to ride."

"You have all that going on at one time?" she asked, starting toward the porch steps.

"Sometimes it can be pretty busy around here," he said, laughing as he opened the front door for her.

When Fee entered and looked around the foyer, she immediately fell in love with Chance's home. The log walls had aged over the years to a beautiful warm honey color and were adorned with pieces of colorful Native American artwork along with cowboy-related items like a pair of well-worn spurs hanging next to a branding iron. Although the Big Blue's main ranch house, where she had attended the wedding, was quite beautiful, it had a more modern feel about it. Chance's home, on the other hand, had that warm, rustic appeal that could only be achieved with the passage of time.

"This is really beautiful," she said, gazing up at the chandelier made of deer antlers. "Did you decorate it?"

"Yeah, I just look like the type of guy who knows all about that stuff, don't I?" Laughing, he shook his head. "After I finished adding on to the cabin and modernizing things like the kitchen and bathrooms, I turned the house over to my mom for the decorating. She has a real knack for that kind of thing."

"Marlene did a wonderful job," Fee said, smiling. "She should have been a professional interior decorator."

"She was too busy chasing a houseful of kids." Before she could ask what he meant, he nodded toward the stairs. "Would you like to see your room?"

"Absolutely," she said as they started upstairs. She couldn't believe how eager she sounded about the bedroom, considering the moment they had just shared out by the truck. To cover the awkwardness, she added, "I can't wait to see what your mother did with the bedrooms."

When they reached the second floor, Chance directed her toward a room at the far end of the hall and opened the door. "If you don't like this one, there are four more you can choose from."

"I love it," Fee said, walking into the cheery room.

The log walls were the same honey color as the ones downstairs, but the room had a more feminine feel to it with the yellow calico curtains and bright patchwork quilt on the log bed. An antique mirror hung on the wall above a cedar-log dresser with a white milk glass pitcher and bowl on top. But her favorite feature of the room had to be the padded window seat beneath the double windows. She could imagine spending rainy afternoons curled up with a good book and a cup of hot peach tea on that bench.

"Your private bathroom is just through there," he said, pointing toward a closed door as he set her luggage on the hardwood plank floor.

"Thank you, Chance." She continued to look around. "This is just fine."

"I'll be downstairs in the kitchen if you need anything. When you get your things unpacked, come on down and we'll see what there is for supper." He stepped closer and lightly touched her cheek with the back of his knuckles. "And just so you know, I am going to do what both of us want."

"W-what's that?" she asked, wondering why the sound of his voice made her feel warm all over.

Her heart skipped a beat when his gaze locked with hers. But when he lightly traced her lower lip with the pad of his thumb, a shiver of anticipation slid up her spine and goose bumps shimmered over her skin.

"I'm going to kiss you, Fee," he said, his tone low and intimate. "And soon." Without another word, he turned and walked out into the hall, closing the door behind him.

Staring after him, she would have liked to deny that he was right about what she wanted. But she couldn't. She had thought he was going to kiss her when he came to get her at the rental house this afternoon and then again when they arrived at the ranch. Both times she'd been disappointed when he hadn't.

With her knees wobbling, she crossed the room to sit on the side of the bed. What on earth had gotten into her? She had a job to do and a promotion to earn. She didn't need the added distraction of a man in her life—even if it was only briefly.

But as she sat there wondering why he was more tempting than any other man she'd ever met, Fee knew without a shadow of a doubt that the chemistry between herself and Chance was going to be extremely hard to resist. Every time he got within ten feet of her, she felt as if the air had been charged by an electric current, and when he touched her, all she could think about was how his lips would feel on hers when he kissed her. She could tell from the looks he gave her and his constant desire to touch her that he was feeling it, as well.

But she had her priorities straight. She was focused on her goal of becoming Lassiter Media's first vice president in charge of public relations under the age of thirty. She wasn't going to risk her career for any man and especially not for a summer fling— even if the sexy-as-sin cowboy had a charming smile and a voice that could melt the polar ice caps.

* * *

"Did you get the little lady squared away?" Gus Swenson asked when Chance entered the kitchen.

Too old to continue doing ranch work and too ornery to go anywhere else, Gus had become the cook and housekeeper after the renovations to the homestead had been completed. If it had been left up to him, Chance would have just had Gus move into the homestead and that would have been that. After all, Gus had been his dad's lifelong best friend—he was practically family. But Gus's pride had been at stake and that's why Chance had disguised his offer in the form of a job. The old man had grumbled about being reduced to doing "women's work," but Chance knew Gus was grateful for the opportunity to live out the rest of his days on the ranch he had worked for the past fifty years.

"Yup. She's in the room across the hall from mine," Chance answered, walking over to hang his hat on a peg beside the back door.

Reaching into the refrigerator, he got himself a beer and popped off the metal cap. He needed something to take the edge off the tension building inside him.

In hindsight, it might not have been the smartest decision he'd ever made to put Fee in the room across from the master suite. If touching her smooth cheek was all it took to make him feel as restless as a bull moose in mating season, how the hell was he going to get any sleep? He tipped the bottle up and drank half the contents. Just the thought of her lying in bed within feet of where he would be, wearing something soft and transparent, her silky blond hair spread across the pillow, had him ready to jump out of his own skin.

"You still got the notion you're gonna talk her outta makin' you a movie star?" Gus asked, drawing him out of his unsettling insight.

"I told you she wants me to be the spokesman for her PR campaign," Chance said, finishing off the beer. "That's a far cry from being in a movie."

"You're gonna be in front of a camera, ain't ya?" Gus asked. Before Chance could answer, the old man went on. "I've got a month's pay that says you'll end up doin' it."

Chance laughed as he tossed the empty bottle in the recycling container under the sink. "That's one bet you'll lose."

The old man grunted. "We'll see, hotshot. You ain't never asked a woman to come stay here before and that's a surefire sign that she's already got you roped. It's just a matter of time before she's got you fallin' all over yourself to do whatever she wants."

Deciding there might be a ring of truth to Gus's observations and not at all comfortable with it, Chance changed the subject. "Did Slim check on the north pasture's grazing conditions today?"

He didn't have to ask if Gus had seen the ranch foreman. The old guy made a trip out to the barn every afternoon when the men came back to the ranch for the day, to shoot the breeze and feel as if he was still a working cowboy.

Gus shook his head. "Slim said they couldn't get to it today. He had to send a couple of the boys over to the west pasture to fix a pretty good stretch of fence that last storm tore up and the rest of 'em were movin' the herd over by the cutbank so they can start mowin' for hay next week."

"I'll take care of it tomorrow," Chance said. He had intended to show Fee around the ranch anyway; he could include the northern section of pasture as part of the tour.

"Something smells absolutely wonderful," she said, walking into the kitchen.

"Thank you, ma'am." Bent over to take a pan of biscuits out of the oven, Gus added, "I don't fix anything real fancy, but I can guarantee it'll taste good and there's plenty of it."

"Fee Sinclair, this is Gus Swenson, the orneriest cowboy this side of the Continental Divide," Chance said, making the introductions.

When Gus straightened and finally turned to face her, Chance watched a slow grin appear on the old man's wrinkled face. "Real nice to meet you, gal." He stood there grinning like a damned fool for several moments before a scowl replaced his easy expression. "Where's your manners, boy? Don't just stand there blinkin' your eyes like a bastard calf in a hailstorm. Offer this little lady a seat while I finish up supper."

"Thank you, but I'd be more than happy to help you finish dinner," Fee offered, smiling.

"I got it all under control, gal," Gus said, reaching into the cabinet to get some plates.

"Could I at least set the table for you?" she asked, walking over to the butcher block island, where Gus had set the plates. "I really do want to help."

Gus looked like a teenage boy with his first crush when he nodded and handed her the dinnerware. "I appreciate it, ma'am."

"Please call me Fee," she said, smiling as she took the plates from the old man.

When she turned toward the table, Gus grinned like a possum and gave Chance a thumbs-up behind her back. "Why don't you make yourself useful, boy? Get some glasses and pour up somethin' for all of us to drink."

As Chance poured three glasses of iced tea and carried them to the table, he couldn't get over the change in Gus. Normally as grouchy as a grizzly bear with a sore paw, the crusty old cowboy was downright pleasant to Fee—at least as close to it as Gus ever got. If he didn't know better, Chance would swear that Gus was smitten.

Twenty minutes later after eating a heaping plate of beef stew, homemade biscuits and a slice of hot apple pie, Chance sat back from the table. "Gus, you outdid yourself. I think that was one of the best meals you've ever made."

"Everything was delicious," Fee agreed, reaching over to cover the old man's hand with hers. "Thank you, Gus."

The gesture caused Gus's cheeks to turn red above

his grizzled beard. "You're more than welcome, gal. Can I get you anything else? Maybe another piece of pie? We got plenty."

Smiling, Fee shook her head. "I couldn't eat another thing. I'm positively stuffed."

Chance rose to take his and Fee's plates to the sink. If anyone was falling all over themselves to do whatever Fee wanted, it was Gus. The old guy was practically begging her to let him do something— anything—for her.

"Would you like to go for a walk after I help Gus clear up the kitchen?" Chance asked, wanting to spend a little time alone with her.

"That would be nice," she said, getting up from the table. "But I want to help with the cleanup first."

"You kids go on and take your walk," Gus said as he got to his feet. "There ain't nothin' much to do but put the leftovers in the refrigerator and load the dishwasher."

"Are you sure, Mr. Swenson?" Fee asked, her voice uncertain.

"The name's Gus, little lady," the old geezer said, grinning from ear to ear. "And I don't mind one bit."

Chance turned to stare at Gus to see if the old man had sprouted another head and a new personality to go with it. He'd never in his entire thirty-two years heard Gus sound so amiable. What was wrong with him?

"Are you feeling all right?" Chance asked, frowning.

"I'm just fine," Gus answered, his smile warning

Chance to drop the matter. "Now, you kids go ahead and take that walk. I'm gonna be turnin' in pretty soon. I'll see you both at breakfast in the mornin'."

Chance shook his head as he reached for his hat hanging on the peg and opened the door. He suddenly knew exactly what was wrong with Gus. Damned if the old fart wasn't trying to play matchmaker.

As they left the house, Fee looked confused. "It's not that late. Is Gus really going to bed this early?"

Chance shook his head. "No, but he's got a set of priorities and in the summer it's baseball. The Rockies are playing the Cardinals on one of the satellite TV channels tonight and he wouldn't miss that for anything. He's going to hole up in his room watching the game."

They fell silent for a moment as they started across the yard toward the barn. "Do you mind if I ask you something, Chance?"

"Not at all. What do you want to know?" he asked, barely resisting the urge to put his arm around her.

To keep from acting on the impulse, he stuffed his hands into the front pockets of his jeans. She had only been on the ranch a couple of hours and he didn't want her to feel as if he was rushing things.

"Earlier this afternoon, you said your mother didn't have time to become an interior decorator because she was too busy chasing after a houseful of children." She paused as if she wasn't sure how to word her question. "I was under the impression that the only sibling you had was your sister."

He nodded. "She is. But up until a couple of months ago, I thought I was an only child."

Fee's confusion was written all over her pretty face. "Am I missing something?"

"Hannah is the product of an affair my dad had when he was out on the rodeo circuit," Chance admitted, still feeling a bit resentful. Although he loved and accepted his half sister, he still struggled with the fact that his father had cheated on his mother. "My mom, dad and uncle J.D. knew about her, but the rest of the family didn't find out until a couple of months ago."

"Okay," Fee said slowly. "But if all your mother had was you, who were the other kids she was running after?"

"Working for Lassiter Media, you've probably heard that Uncle J.D.'s wife died within a few days of having Angelica." When Fee nodded, he continued, "Uncle J.D. had his hands full trying to raise three little kids on his own. Mom helped out as much as she could, but she had me and Dad to take care of and was only able to do so much. Then after my dad got killed four years later, my uncle suggested that Mom and I move into the main house with him and his kids. By that time he had opened the Lassiter Media office in L.A. and traveled back and forth a lot. He needed someone he trusted to take care of his kids and my mom was the obvious choice. She knew and loved the kids and they all considered her a second mother anyway."

"That makes sense," she agreed. "Was your parents' home nearby?"

"We lived here at the homestead." He couldn't help but feel a strong sense of pride that he was the third generation to own this section of the ranch. "My dad was more of a cowboy than Uncle J.D. ever thought about being and when he wasn't riding the rough stock in a rodeo somewhere, Dad was working here at the ranch. After my uncle built the main house, Uncle J.D. gave this part of the Big Blue to us."

"No wonder the family is extremely close," Fee said thoughtfully. "Sage, Dylan and Angelica are more like your siblings than they are cousins."

As they walked into the barn, Chance gave in to temptation and casually draped his arm across her slender shoulders. She gave him a sideways glance, but he took it as a good sign that she didn't protest.

"The only time the four of us weren't together was at night when we went to bed," he explained. "Uncle J.D. gave my mom and me one wing of the house so that we would have our privacy, while he and his kids took the other wing."

"You must have had a wonderful childhood with other children to play with," Fee said, sounding wistful.

"I can't complain," he admitted. "What about your family? Do you have a brother or sister?"

She shook her head. "I was an only child."

When she failed to elaborate, Chance decided to let the matter drop. It was clear she didn't want to talk about it and he'd never been one to pry. If Fee wanted to tell him about her family, he would be more than happy to listen. If she didn't, then that was her call.

Walking down the long aisle between the horse stalls, Chance pointed to a paint mare that had curiously poked her head over the bottom half of the stall door. "That's the horse you'll learn to ride tomorrow."

Fee looked uncertain. "It looks so big. Do you have one in a smaller size?"

"You make it sound like you're trying on a pair of shoes," he said, laughing. "Rosy is about as small as we have around here."

"I'm not so comfortable with large animals," she said, shaking her head. "When I was little girl, my grandmother's next door neighbor had an overly friendly Great Dane that knocked me down every time I was around him. I know he wasn't trying to hurt me, but I ended up with stitches in my knee from his friendly gestures." She eyed the mare suspiciously. "She's bigger than he was."

He guided Fee over to the stall. "I promise Rosy is the gentlest horse we have on the ranch and loves people." Reaching out, he scratched the mare's forehead. "She'll be the perfect starter horse for you and she won't knock you down."

"Rosy likes that?" Fee asked.

He nodded. "You want to try it?" When she shook her head, he took her hand in his. "Just rub Rosy's forehead like this," he said, showing her how. "While you two get acquainted, I'll go get a treat for you to feed her."

"I don't think that's a good idea, Chance." He heard the hesitancy in her voice as he walked across the aisle into the feed room. "She looks like she might have pretty big teeth. Does she bite?"

He shook his head as he walked back to the stall with a cube of sugar. "Rosy might nip you unintentionally, but she's never been one to bite." He placed the cube on Fee's palm. "Just keep your hand flat and Rosy will take care of the rest."

When Fee tentatively put her hand out, the mare scooped up the sugar cube with her lips. "Oh my goodness!" Fee's expression was filled with awe when she turned to look at him. "Her mouth is so soft. It feels just like velvet."

Seeing the wonder in her eyes and her delighted smile, Chance didn't think twice about closing the gap between them to take Fee in his arms. "Do you remember what I told you this afternoon?"

The glee in her vibrant blue eyes changed to the awareness he'd seen in them earlier in the day. "Y-yes."

"Good." He started to lower his head and was encouraged when she brought her arms up to encircle his neck. "I'm going to give you that kiss now that we've both been wanting."

When he covered her mouth with his, Chance didn't think he had ever tasted anything sweeter. He took his time to slowly, thoroughly explore her soft lips. They were perfect and clung to his as if she was eager for him to take the kiss to the next level. When she sighed and melted into him, he didn't think twice about tightening his arms around her and deepening the caress.

The moment his tongue touched hers, Chance felt a wave of heat shoot from the top of his head all the way to the soles of his feet. But when she slid her hands beneath the collar of his shirt to caress the nape of his neck, it felt as if his heart turned a somersault inside his chest. The magnetic pull between them was more explosive than anything he could have imagined and he knew as surely as he knew his own name it was inevitable—they would be making love. The thought caused the region south of his belt buckle to tighten so fast it left him feeling lightheaded.

Easing away from the kiss before things got out of hand, he gazed down at the dazed expression on her pretty face. She was as turned on as he was and, unless he missed his guess, a little confused by how quickly the passion had flared between them.

"I think we'd better call it a night," he said, continuing to hold her.

"I-it would…probably be a good…idea," she said, sounding as breathless as he felt.

"Mornings around here start earlier than you're probably used to," he advised, forcing himself to take a step back.

When he put his arm around her and started walking toward the open doors of the barn, she asked, "How early are we talking about?"

He grinned. "Well before daylight."

"Is it that imperative to get up so early?" she asked, frowning.

"The livestock get breakfast before we do," he explained, holding her to his side. "Besides, in the summer we get as much done as we can before the hottest part of the day. The earlier we get up and get started, the better chance we have of doing that."

"I suppose that makes sense," she said as they climbed the porch steps and went into the house. "Why don't you wake me up when you get back to the house after you feed the livestock?"

"Hey, you're the one who's here to observe what a real cowboy is all about," he reminded, laughing. "That includes the morning chores as well as what I do the rest of the day."

"No, I'm here to talk you into being the spokesman for your family's PR campaign," she shot back. "It was your idea that I needed to see what you do."

Walking her into the foyer of the homestead and up the stairs, they fell silent and Chance cursed himself as nine kinds of a fool the closer they got to their bedrooms. After he had put her in the room across the hall from his, he'd realized that it probably hadn't been one of his brightest ideas. But now that he knew the sweetness of her lips and how responsive she was to his kiss, there wasn't a doubt in his mind that it was the dumbest decision he'd made in his entire adult life. But at the time, he'd thought she might like the room with the window seat. It was the only one of the six bedrooms that was the least bit feminine.

When they stopped at the door to her room, he barely resisted the temptation of taking her back into his arms. "Sleep well, Fee."

"You, too, Chance," she said, giving him a smile that sent his blood pressure skyrocketing.

He waited until she went into her room, then quickly entering his, he closed the door and headed straight for the shower. Between the kiss they'd shared in the barn and the knowledge that at that very moment she was probably removing every stitch of clothes she had on, he was hotter than a two-dollar pistol in a skid-row pawn shop on Saturday night.

He'd have liked nothing more than to hold Fee to him and kiss her senseless. But that hadn't been an option. If he had so much as touched her, he knew he wouldn't have wanted to let her go. And that had never happened to him before.

It wasn't as if he hadn't experienced a strong attraction for a woman in the past. But nothing in his adult life had been as passionate as fast as what he had felt with Fee when he kissed her. He hadn't counted on that when he asked her to stay with him. Hell, the possibility hadn't even been on his radar.

Quickly stripping out of his clothes, he turned on the water and stepped beneath the icy spray. Maybe if he traumatized his body with a cold shower, he'd not only be able to get some sleep, maybe some of his sanity would return.

As he stood there shivering uncontrollably, he shook his head. Yeah, and if he believed that, there was someone, somewhere waiting to sell him the Grand Canyon or Mount Rushmore.

Four

Fee yawned as she sat on a bale of hay in the barn and watched Chance saddle Rosy and another horse he'd called Dakota. She couldn't believe that after he'd knocked on her door an hour and a half before the sun came up, he'd gone on to feed all of the animals housed in the barns and holding pens and met with his ranch foreman to go over the chores for the day—all before breakfast.

Hiding another yawn with her hand, she decided she might not be as tired if she'd gotten more rest the night before. But sleep had eluded her and she knew exactly what had caused her insomnia. Not only had Chance's kiss been way more than she'd expected, it had caused her to question her sanity.

Several different times yesterday, she had practically asked the man to kiss her and when he finally had, she'd acted completely shameless and all but melted into a puddle at his big booted feet. Thank goodness he'd kept it fairly brief and ended the kiss before she'd made a bigger fool of herself than she already had.

Then there was the matter of the promise she'd made to herself years ago. She'd seemed to forget all about her vow to never put her career in jeopardy because of a man.

"You're not your mother," she whispered to herself.

Her mother had been a prime example of how that kind of diversion could destroy a career, and Fee was determined not to let that happen to her. Rita Sinclair had abandoned her position as a successful financial advisor when she foolishly fell head over heels in love with a dreamer—a man who chased his lofty ideas from one place to another without ever considering the sacrifices his aspirations had cost her. Maybe he'd asked her to marry him because she had become pregnant with Fee or maybe he'd thought it was what he wanted at the time. Either way, he had eventually decided that his wife and infant daughter were holding him back and he'd moved on without them.

But instead of picking up the pieces of her life and resuming her career, Fee's mother had settled for working one dead-end job after another that left her with little time for her daughter. Her mother had died ten years ago, still waiting for the dreamer to return to take her with him on his next irresponsible adventure. Fee suspected that her mother had died of a broken heart because he never did.

When she'd been old enough to understand the life her mother had given up for her father, Fee had made a conscious decision to avoid making the same mistakes.

Although he wasn't her boss, Chance's family owned the company she worked for and that was even worse. She could very easily end up getting herself fired.

She tried to think if she'd heard anything about Lassiter Media's policy on fraternization. Would that even apply in this situation? Chance wasn't an employee of the company, nor was he an owner. But he was closely related to those who were and she'd been sent to smooth over a scandal, not create another one.

"I don't know what you're thinking, but if that frown on your face is any indication, it can't be good," Chance said, breaking into her disturbing thoughts.

"I was thinking about the PR campaign," she answered, staring down at the toes of her new boots. "I should be working on ideas for the videos and print ads."

Technically it wasn't really a lie. She had been thinking about the reasons she'd been sent to Wyoming and how losing her focus when it came to him could very easily cost her a perfectly good job.

Squatting down in front of her, Chance used his index finger to lift her chin until their gazes met.

"What do you say we forget about fixing the Lassiter reputation today and just have a little fun?"

The moment he touched her, Fee could barely remember her own name, let alone the fact that she had a job she might lose if she wasn't careful. "You think I'm going to have fun riding a horse?" she asked, unable to keep the skepticism from her voice.

"I promise you will," he said, taking her hands in his. Straightening to his full height, he pulled her to her feet, then picked up her hat where she had placed it on the bale of hay when she sat down. Positioning it on her head, he pointed to Rosy. "Now, are you ready to mount up and get started?"

"Not really," she said, wondering if workers' compensation would cover her falling off a horse since she was only learning to ride in an effort to get him to agree to be the Lassiter spokesman. Eying the mare, Fee shook her head. "Is it just me or did she get a lot bigger overnight?"

"It's just you," he said, laughing as he led her over to the mare's side. He explained how to put her foot in the stirrup and take hold of the saddle to pull herself up onto the back of the horse. "Don't worry about Rosy. She's been trained to stand perfectly still until you're seated and give her the signal you're ready for her to move."

"It's the after I'm seated part that I'm worried about," Fee muttered as she took a deep breath and barely managed to raise her foot high enough to place it in the stirrup. Grabbing the saddle as Chance had instructed, she tried to mount the horse but found the task impossible. "How is stepping into the stirrup any help when your knee is even with your chin?" she asked, feeling relief flow through her. If she couldn't mount the horse, she couldn't ride it. "I guess I won't be able to go riding. At least not until you get a shorter horse."

"It takes a little practice," he answered, grinning. "Besides, the horse isn't as tall as you are short."

She shook her head. "There's nothing wrong with being short."

"I didn't say there was," he said, stepping behind her.

Fee's heart felt as if it stopped, then took off at a gallop when, without warning, he placed one hand at her waist and the other on the seat of her new jeans. Before she could process what was taking place, Chance boosted her up into the saddle. Her cheeks heated and she wasn't sure if it was from embarrassment or the awareness coursing through her.

But when she realized she was actually sitting atop Rosy, Fee forgot all about sorting out her reaction to Chance. Wrapping both hands around the saddle horn, she held on for dear life. "This is even higher than I thought it would be. I really do think a shorter horse would work out a lot better."

"Try to relax and sit naturally," he coaxed. He reached up to gently pry her hands from the saddle. "You don't want to be as stiff as a ramrod."

When the mare shifted her weight from one foot to the other, Fee scrunched her eyes shut and waited for the worst. "I thought you said she would stand still."

"Fee, look at me," he commanded. When she opened first one eye and then the other, the promise in his brilliant green eyes stole her breath. "Do you trust me?"

"Yes." She wasn't sure why, given that she hadn't known him all that long, but she did trust him.

"I give you my word that I won't let anything happen to you," he assured her. "You're completely safe, sweetheart."

Her heart stalled and she suddenly found it hard to draw a breath. The sound of his deep voice when he used the endearment caused heat to fill her. Why did she suddenly wish he was talking about something besides riding a horse?

Unable to get her vocal cords to work, she simply nodded.

"Good." He checked to make sure the stirrups were adjusted to the right length. "Now I want you to slightly tilt your heels down just below horizontal."

"Why?" she asked even as she followed his instructions.

"Shifting your weight to your heels instead of the balls of your feet helps you relax your legs and sit more securely," he explained. "And it's more natural and comfortable for both you and Rosy." He took hold of the mare's reins, then reached for his horse's reins, as well. "Now are you ready to go for your first ride?"

"Would it make a difference if I said no?" she asked, already knowing the answer.

Grinning, he shook his head. "Nope."

"I didn't think so." Fee caught her breath when the mare slowly started walking beside Chance as he led both horses out of the barn. But instead of the bumpy ride she expected, it was more of a smooth rocking motion. "This isn't as rough as I thought it would be."

"It isn't when you relax and move with the horse, instead of against it," he said, leading them over to the round pen he had mentioned was used for training. Once he had his horse tied to the outside of the fence, he opened the gate and led the mare inside. "Hold the reins loosely," he said, handing Fee the leather straps. He walked around the pen beside Rosy until they had made a complete circle. "Now, I'm going to stand right here while you and Rosy go around."

A mixture of adrenaline and fear rose inside of Fee like a Pacific tsunami. "What am I supposed to do?"

"Just sit there and let Rosy do the rest," he said calmly. "I promise you'll be fine."

As the horse carried her around the enclosure, Fee noticed that the mare kept turning her head to look back at her. "Yes, Rosy, I'm scared witless. Please prove Chance right and don't do anything I'll regret."

To her surprise the mare snorted and bobbed her head up and down as if she understood what Fee had requested as she continued to slowly walk around the inside of the fence.

By the time Rosy had made her way back around to the gate for the second time, Fee began to feel a little more confident. "This isn't as difficult as I thought it would be."

"It's not," Chance said when the mare stopped in front of him. "Are you ready to take a tour of the ranch now?" he asked, patting the mare's sleek neck.

"I…guess so," Fee answered, not at all sure she was ready to ride outside of the enclosure. But Rosy seemed to be willing and Fee felt some of her usual self-confidence begin to return.

"Don't worry," Chance said, as if reading her mind. He opened the gate to lead the mare out. "Rosy is kid broke and you're doing great for your first time on a horse."

Fee frowned. "What does kid broke mean?"

"Her temperament and training make her safe enough to let a little kid ride her with minimal risk of anything happening," he said, mounting his horse. "And I'll be right beside you."

As they rode across the pasture and headed toward a hillside in the distance, she reflected on how far out of her element she was. Up until today, her idea of adventure had been a shopping trip to one of the malls in the San Fernando Valley the day after Thanksgiving.

But she had to admit that riding a horse wasn't as bad as she thought it would be. In fact, the more she thought about it, the more she realized she was actu-

ally enjoying the experience. And if that wasn't un-
usual enough, they were traveling across a deserted
expanse of land where wild animals roamed free and
she wasn't all that afraid of being something's next
meal. Unbelievable!

Fee glanced over at the man riding beside her.
What was it about Chance that could get her to do
things that were totally out of character for her and
without much protest on her part?

Staring out across the land, she knew exactly why
she was willing to step out of her comfort zone and
try new things. She trusted Chance—trusted that he
wouldn't ask anything of her that she couldn't do and
wouldn't allow anything to harm her.

The realization caused her heart to skip a beat.
She didn't trust easily and especially when it came
to men. The fact that she had already placed her faith
in Chance was more than a little disturbing. Why
was he different?

It could have something to do with the fact that
so far, he was exactly what he said he was—a hard-
working rancher who was more interested in drawing attention to the quality of the beef he raised than
being in the limelight himself. Or maybe it was the
fact that he was vastly different from any of the men
she knew in L.A. Although great guys, most of them
would rather sit behind a desk in a climate-controlled
office than be outside getting their hands dirty.

She wasn't sure why she trusted Chance, but one
thing was certain: she was going to have to be on

her guard at all times. Otherwise, she just might find herself falling for him and end up out of a job.

As they rode up the trail leading to the north pasture, Chance was proud of the way Fee had taken to horseback riding. At first, she had been extremely apprehensive about getting on a horse, but she'd at least had the guts to try. That was something he admired.

In fact, there were a lot of things about her that he appreciated. She was not only courageous, she was dedicated. He didn't know any other woman who would go to the lengths she had in her effort to do her job and do it right. Fee was willing to do whatever it took to get him to agree to be the spokesman in her ad campaign, even if that meant getting up at a time most city dwellers thought was the middle of the night and riding a horse for the first time. And from what Sage had told him, she was sensitive to others. Apparently, Colleen had tentatively offered to let Fee use their upcoming wedding as part of the PR campaign to improve the Lassiters' image, but she hadn't wanted to exploit their big day and had politely declined.

"Rosy and I seem to be getting along pretty well," Fee said, bringing him back to the present.

"So you're having a good time?" he asked, noticing how silky her hair looked as a light breeze played with the blond strands of her ponytail.

"Yes," she said, giving him a smile. "I didn't think

I would, but I really am. Of course, I might not feel the same way if I was riding a different horse."

"I was pretty sure you and Rosy were…a good match," he said, distracted by the faint sound of a cow bawling in the distance. Staring in the direction the sound came from, he spotted a large black cow lying on her side about two hundred yards away. It was clear the animal was in distress. "Damn!"

"What happened?" Fee asked, looking alarmed.

"I'm going to have to ride on ahead," he said quickly. "You'll be fine. I'll be within sight and Rosy will bring you right to me."

Before Fee had the chance to question him further or protest that he was leaving her behind, he kicked Dakota into a gallop and raced toward the cow. The bay gelding covered the distance quickly and when he reached the cow, Chance could tell that not only was she in labor, she was having trouble delivering the calf.

Dismounting, he immediately started rolling up the long sleeves on his chambray shirt. He could tell from her shallow breathing that the animal had been at this awhile and was extremely weak. He was going to have to see what the problem was, then try to do what he could to help. Otherwise there was a very real possibility he would lose both the heifer and her calf.

"What's wrong with it?" Fee asked when she and Rosy finally reached the spot where the cow lay.

"I'm pretty sure the calf is hung up," he said, taking off his wristwatch and slipping it into the front pocket of his jeans. He reached into the saddlebags tied behind Dakota's saddle and removed a packet of disinfectant wipes.

Fee looked genuinely concerned. "Oh, the poor thing. Is there anything you can do to help her? Should you call the veterinarian?"

"The vet will take too long to get here." Walking over to the mare, he lifted Fee down from the saddle and set her on her feet. "I'm going to need you to hold the heifer's tail while I check to see what the problem is," he said, taking several of the wet cloths from the packet to wipe down his hands and arms. "Do you think you can do that, Fee?"

He could tell she wasn't at all sure about getting that close to the animal, but she took a deep breath and nodded. "I'll do my best."

"Good." He couldn't stop himself from giving her a quick kiss. Then catching the cow's wildly switching tail, he handed it to Fee. "Hold on tight while I see if the calf's breech or it's just too big."

While Fee held the tail out of the way, Chance knelt down at the back of the animal. He wished that he had some of the shoulder-length gloves from one of the calving sheds back at ranch headquarters, but since that wasn't an option, he gritted his teeth and proceeded to do what he could to help the heifer. Reaching inside, he felt the calf, and sure enough, one of the legs was folded at the knee. Pushing the calf back, he carefully straightened its front leg, then gently but firmly pulled it back into the birth position.

"Will she be able to have the calf now?" Fee asked, her tone anxious as she let go of the tail and put distance between herself and the cow.

"I hope so," he said, rising to his feet. Using more of the wipes, he cleaned his arm as he waited to see if the heifer was going to be able to calve. "I'll have to check my records when I get back to the house, but I'm pretty sure this is her first calf."

When the cow made an odd noise, Fee looked worried. "Is she all right?"

"She's pretty tired, but we should know within a few minutes if she'll be able to do this on her own," he said, focusing on the cow to see if there were any more signs of distress. When he saw none, he walked over to Fee.

"And if she can't?" Fee asked.

"Then I become a bovine obstetrician and help her out," he answered, shrugging. "It wouldn't be the first time and it won't be the last."

"This is definitely one of those jobs you mentioned that most people would consider disgusting."

"Yup." He noticed the heifer was starting to work with her contractions and that was a good sign she at least wasn't too exhausted to try.

"Maybe a lot of people find something like this distasteful, but I think it's rather heroic," Fee said, thoughtfully. "You care enough about the animals on this ranch to make sure they're well taken care of and if that means getting your hands dirty to save one of them or to help relieve their suffering, then that's what you do."

He nodded. "I'm responsible for them and that includes keeping them healthy."

Chance had never really thought about his job the way Fee had just pointed out. Sure, he liked animals—liked working with them and being around them. He wouldn't be much of a rancher if he didn't. But he had never really thought about what he did as heroic. To him, taking good care of his livestock was not just part of the job description, it was the right thing to do.

"Oh my goodness," Fee said suddenly when the calf began to emerge from the cow. Her expression was filled with awe. "This is amazing."

Confident that the animal was going to be able to have the calf without further intervention on his part, he used his cell phone to call ranch headquarters. He needed to get one of his men to come out and watch over the heifer until she and the calf could be moved to one of the holding pens close to the barn.

When the calf slid out onto the ground, Chance walked over to make sure it was breathing and checked it over while the heifer rested. "It's a girl," he said, grinning as he walked back to Fee.

"Is the momma cow going to be all right?" Fee asked.

He nodded as he draped his arm across her shoulders. "I think she'll be just fine. But Slim is sending one of the boys out here to see that she gets back to the ranch, where we can watch her and she can rest up a little. Then she and her baby will rejoin the herd in a few days."

Fee frowned. "Why was she out here by herself to begin with?"

"Livestock have a tendency to want to go off by themselves when they're in labor," Chance explained.

"For privacy." She nodded. "I can understand that."

He watched the cow get up and nudge her baby with her nose, urging it to stand, as well. "She had probably done that yesterday when the men moved the herd and they just missed seeing her. Normally, our cattle calve in the spring, but she apparently got bred later than usual, throwing her having her calf to now."

"But they will be back at the ranch house and I'll be able to see the calf again?" she asked, looking hopeful as, after several attempts, the calf gained her footing and managed to stand.

"Sure, you'll be able to see her." He grinned. "But I somehow got the impression you didn't like big animals all that much and might even be a little afraid of them."

"This one is different," she insisted, her voice softening when the calf wobbled over to her mother and started to nurse. "It's a baby and not all that big yet. Besides, the fence will be between me and her momma."

Seeing the cowboy he'd called for riding toward them, Chance led Fee over to Rosy. "Our replacement is almost here. Are you ready to mount up and finish checking on the grazing conditions before we head back to the house?"

"I suppose," she said, lifting her foot to put it into the stirrup. "This would be a whole lot easier if Rosy was shorter."

As he stepped up behind her, Chance took a deep breath and got ready to give her a boost up into the saddle. Touching her cute little backside when she'd mounted the mare the first time had damn near caused him to have a coronary. He could only guess what his reaction would be this time.

The minute his palm touched the seat of her blue jeans, a jolt of electric current shot up his arm, down through his chest and straight to the region south of his belt buckle. His reaction was not only predictable, it was instantaneous.

Feeling as if his own jeans had suddenly gotten a couple of sizes smaller in the stride, he waited to make sure Fee was settled on Rosy before he caught Dakota's reins in one hand and gingerly swung up onto the gelding's saddle. He immediately shifted to keep from emasculating himself. Fee hadn't been on the ranch a full twenty-four hours and he was already in need of a second cold shower.

As they started toward the north pasture, Chance decided it was either going to be the most exciting two weeks of his life or the most grueling. And he had every intention of seeing that it was going to be the former, not the latter.

While Chance called his mother to make arrangements to take Cassie for ice cream the next day, Fee helped clean the kitchen after dinner. "Gus, it was the most amazing thing I've ever seen. He knew exactly what to do and everything turned out fine for the momma cow, as well as for her baby."

She still couldn't get over the efficiency and expertise Chance had demonstrated with the pregnant cow. What he'd had to do to help the animal was messy and disgusting, but he hadn't hesitated for a single second. He had immediately sprung into action and taken care of her and her calf to make sure they both survived.

It was hard to believe how many facets there were to Chance's job. He not only had to keep extensive records on all of the livestock, he had to be a land manager, an experienced horseman and an impromptu large-animal veterinarian. And she had a feeling that was just the tip of the iceberg.

"Don't go tellin' him I said so 'cause I don't want him gettin' bigheaded about it," Gus said, grinning. "But that boy's got better cow sense than even his daddy had. And that's sayin' somethin'. When Charlie Lassiter was alive there was none better at ranchin' than he was. He knew what a steer was gonna do before it did."

Fee remembered Chance telling her that his father had run the ranch when he wasn't out on the rodeo circuit. "How did Chance's father die? Was he killed at a rodeo?"

"It was one of them freak accidents that never shoulda happened." Gus shook his head sadly as he handed her a pot he had just finished washing. "Charlie was a saddle bronc and bareback rider when he was out on the rodeo circuit, and a damned good one. He always finished in the money and other than a busted arm one time, never got hurt real bad. But about three years after he stopped rodeoin' and went to ranchin' full time, he got throwed from a horse he was breakin'. He landed wrong and it snapped his neck. Charlie was dead as soon as he hit the ground."

"That's so sad," she said, drying the pot with a soft cotton dish towel before hanging it on the pot rack above the kitchen island.

"The real bad thing was Chance saw it all," Gus said, his tone turning husky.

"Oh, how awful!" Fee gasped.

Gus nodded. "After Charlie started bein' at home all the time, that little kid was his daddy's shadow and followed him everywhere. It weren't no surprise to any of us that Chance was sittin' on the top fence rail watchin' Charlie that day."

Fee's heart broke for Chance and it took a moment for her to be able to speak around the lump clogging her throat. "How old…was Chance?"

"That was twenty-four years ago," Gus answered. He cleared his throat as if he was having just as hard a time speaking as she was. "That would have made Chance about eight."

She couldn't stop tears from filling her eyes when she thought about Chance as a little boy watching the father he idolized die. Although she'd never really known her father and hadn't been all that close to her mother, she couldn't imagine watching someone she loved so much die in such a tragic way. That had to have been devastating for him.

"Well, that's taken care of," Chance said, walking into the room. He had called his mother to let her know what time they would be stopping by the main house tomorrow to take his niece to get ice cream. Marlene was keeping Cassie while Hannah and Logan were on their honeymoon, and she could probably use a break. "Mom said she would have Cassie ready tomorrow afternoon for us to come by and get her."

Without thinking, Fee walked over and wrapped her arms around his waist to give him a hug. She knew he would probably think she'd lost her mind, but she didn't care. The more she found out about Chance Lassiter the more she realized what a remarkable man he was. He'd suffered through a traumatic loss as a child, but that hadn't deterred him from following in his father's footsteps to become a rancher. And from what she'd seen at the wedding a few nights ago, he had gone out of his way to become close to the half sister and niece that he hadn't even known existed until just recently.

"Don't get me wrong, sweetheart," he said, chuckling as his arms closed around her. "I'm not complaining in the least, but what's this for?"

Knowing that if she tried to explain her actions, she'd make a fool of herself, she shrugged and took a step back. "I'm still amazed that you knew what to do today to save the momma cow and her baby."

He smiled. "How would you like to take a walk out to the holding pen to check on them?"

"I'd like that," she said, meaning it. "Gus and I just finished up the dishes."

Gus nodded. "I'll see you at breakfast. I've a baseball game comin' on the sports channel in a few minutes."

As Gus went to his room to watch the game, she and Chance left the house and walked across the yard toward the barn. She glanced up at him when he reached out and took her hand in his. It was a small gesture, but the fact that it felt so good to have him touch her, even in such a small way, was a little unsettling. Was she already in way over her head?

"Looks like we may have to cut our walk short," Chance said, pointing to a bank of clouds in the distance. "We might get a little rain."

"From the dark color, I'd say it's going to be a downpour," Fee commented as they reached the pen where the cow and calf were being held.

"Even if it is a downpour, it probably won't last long," he answered. "We get a lot of pop-up thundershowers this time of year. They move through, dump a little water on us and move on."

Noticing a covered area at one end of the enclosure, she nodded. "I'm glad to see there's shelter for them if it does start raining."

"Cattle don't usually mind being out in the rain during the summer months," he said, smiling. "It's one of the ways they cool off."

"What's another?" she asked, watching the little black calf venture away from her mother.

"If there's a pond or a river, they like to wade out and just stand there." He grinned. "Sort of like the bovine version of skinny-dipping."

"I can't say I blame them," she said, laughing. "I would think it gets rather hot with all that hair." When the calf got close to the fence, Fee couldn't help but feel a sense of awe. "She's so pretty. What are you going to name her?"

He chuckled. "We normally don't name cattle."

"I guess that would be kind of difficult when you have so many," she said, thinking it was a shame for something so cute not to have a name.

He nodded. "If they're going to be kept for breeding purposes, we tag their ears with a number. That's the way we identify them and keep track of their health and how well they do during calving season."

"I don't care," Fee said, looking into the baby's big brown eyes. "She's too cute to just be a number. I'm going to call her Belle."

"So before we take her and her mother to rejoin the herd, I should have her name put on her ear tag instead of a number?" he asked, grinning as he reached out and caught her to him.

She placed her hands on his chest and started to tell him that was exactly what she thought he should do, but she stopped short when several fat raindrops landed on her face. "We'll be soaked to the bone by the time we get back to the house," she said when it started raining harder.

Chance grabbed hold of her hand and pulled her along in the direction of the barn. "We can wait it out in there."

Sprinting the short distance, a loud clap of thunder echoed overhead as they ran inside. "That rain moved in fast," she said, laughing.

"Unless it's a big storm front, it should move through just as fast." He stared at her for several seconds before he took her by the hand and led her midway down the long center aisle to a narrow set of stairs on the far side of the feed room. "There's something I want to show you."

When he stepped back for her to precede him up the steps, she frowned. "What is it?"

"Trust me, you'll like it," he said, smiling mysteriously.

"I'm sure that's what a spider says to a fly just before it lures him into its web," she said, looking up the stairs to the floor above. She didn't know what he had up his sleeve, but she did trust him and smiling over her shoulder at him, climbed the stairs to the hayloft. When they stood facing each other at the top of the stairs, she asked, "Now, what is it you wanted to show me?"

He walked her over to the open doors at the end of the loft. "We'll have to wait until it stops raining and the sun comes back out," he said, taking her into his arms.

A shiver coursed through her and not entirely from her rain-dampened clothes. The look in Chance's eyes stole her breath and sent waves of goose bumps shimmering over her skin.

"Chance, I don't think this is a good idea," she warned. "I'm not interested in an involvement."

He shook his head. "I'm not, either. All I want is for both of us to enjoy your visit to the ranch."

"I need to talk to you about the PR campaign," she said, reminding him that she wasn't giving up on him being the family spokesman.

He nodded. "I promise we'll get to that soon. But right now, I'm going to kiss you again, Fee," he said, lowering his head. "And this time it's going to be a long, slow kiss that will leave both of us gasping for breath."

Fee's heart pounded hard in her chest when his mouth covered hers and a delicious heat began to spread throughout her body as she raised her arms to encircle his neck. True to his word, Chance took his time, teasing with tiny nibbling kisses that heightened her anticipation, and when he finally traced her lips with his tongue to deepen the caress, Fee felt as if she would go into total meltdown.

As he explored her slowly, thoroughly, he slid his hand from her back up along her ribs to the underside of her breast. Cupping her, he lightly teased the hardened tip with the pad of his thumb and even through the layers of her clothing the sensation was electrifying. A lazy tightening began to form a coil in the pit of her stomach and she instinctively leaned into his big, hard body.

The feel of his rigid arousal nestled against her

soft lower belly, the tightening of his strong arms around her and the feel of his heart pounding out a steady rhythm against her breast sent a need like nothing she had ever known flowing from the top of her head all the way to the soles of her feet.

Her knees wobbled, then failed her completely as he continued to stroke her with a tenderness that brought tears to her eyes. She had been kissed before, but nothing like this. It felt as if she had been waiting on this man and this moment her entire life.

The thought frightened her as little else could. Pushing against his chest, she took a step back to stare up at him. "I'm not good at playing games, Chance."

"I'm not asking you to play games, Fee." He shook his head. "We can have fun while you're here, and when you go back to L.A., you'll have the memory of the good time we had. As long as we keep that in mind, we should be just fine."

She stared at him for several long seconds as she waged a battle within herself. He wasn't asking for anything more from her than the here and now. But there was one problem with his reasoning. She wasn't entirely certain she could trust her heart to listen. Lowering his head, he kissed her again.

"I do believe, Fee Sinclair, that you have the sweetest lips of any woman I've ever known," he whispered close to her ear.

Another tremor of desire slid through her a moment before he pulled back and pointed toward the open doors of the loft. "This is what I wanted you to see."

Looking in the direction he indicated, Fee caught her breath. A brilliantly colored full rainbow arched across the bluest sky she had ever seen.

"It's gorgeous," she murmured.

"Did you know that in some cultures the rainbow symbolizes a new beginning or a new phase in a person's life?" he asked, kissing her forehead as he held her to him and they watched the vibrant prism fade away.

She swallowed hard as she turned her attention to the man holding her close. What was it about being wrapped in Chance's arms that made her feel as if she was entering a new phase in her life—one that she hadn't seen coming and was powerless to stop? And one that made her extremely uneasy.

Five

Standing at the ice-cream counter in Buckaroo Billy's General Store on the outskirts of Cheyenne, Chance glanced through the window at Fee and his niece seated under a big yellow umbrella at one of the picnic tables outside. Cassie was talking a mile a minute and it seemed that Fee was somehow keeping up. That in itself was pretty darned amazing. The kid usually had him confused as hell by the speed she changed subjects. He loved her dearly, but sometimes Cassie had the attention span of a flea and hopped from one topic to another faster than a drop of water on a hot griddle.

Paying for their ice cream, he juggled the three cones and a handful of paper napkins as he shouldered open the door. "A scoop of chocolate fudge brownie for you, princess," he said, handing Cassie the frozen treat. Turning to Fee, he grinned. "And mint chocolate chip for you."

"Uncle Chance!" Cassie exclaimed, pointing to his vanilla ice cream. "You were supposed to try something new this time."

"Where's your sense of adventure, Mr. Lassiter?" Fee asked, laughing.

"I like vanilla," he said, shrugging as he dropped the napkins onto the table and sat down. He should have known Cassie would remember he was supposed to try a new flavor. The kid had a mind like a steel trap. Grinning, he added, "But next week, I promise I'll leave what I get up to you two. How does that sound?"

Cassie's red curls bobbed when she nodded her approval. "I like that. I'll ask Momma what you should have when she gets home." True to form, she looked at Fee and took the conversation in another direction. "My mommy and daddy are on their moneyhoon. That's why I'm staying with Grandma Marlene."

"You mean honeymoon?" Chance asked, winking at Fee. He could tell she was trying hard not to laugh at Cassie's mix-up, the same as he was.

"Yeah. They went on a boat." Cassie shook her head. "But I don't know where."

"After much debate, Hannah and Logan went on a Caribbean cruise," Chance explained to Fee.

She smiled at his niece. "That sounds like a nice honeymoon."

"They're going to bring me back a present," Cassie added as she licked some of the chocolate dripping onto her fingers. When she started to touch her tongue to the ice cream in her usual exuberant fashion, the scoop dislodged from the cone and landed on the top of her tennis shoe. Tears immediately filled her big green eyes and her little chin began to wobble. "I'm sorry. It…fell…Uncle Chance."

"Don't cry, princess," he said gently as he reached over and gave her a hug. "It's all right. I'll get you another one."

While Fee used the napkins to clean off Cassie's shoe, he went back into the store to replace her ice-cream cone. By the time he returned a couple of minutes later, Cassie was all smiles and chattering like a magpie once again.

His mind wandered as his niece and Fee discussed the newest version of a popular fashion doll—and he couldn't help but notice every time Fee licked her ice cream.

"Chance, did you hear me?" Fee asked, sounding concerned.

"Oh, sorry." He grinned. "I was still thinking about doll accessories."

She gave him one of those looks that women were so fond of when they thought a man was full of bull roar. "I said I'm going to take Cassie to the ladies' room to wash her hands."

He nodded. "Good idea."

As he watched Fee and his niece walk into the store, he shook his head at his own foolishness and rose to his feet to walk over to his truck to wait for them to return. If he and Fee didn't make love soon, he was going to be a raving lunatic.

But as he stood there thinking about the danger to his mental health, he realized that making love with Fee wasn't all he wanted. The thought caused his heart to pound hard against his ribs. He wasn't thinking about an actual relationship, was he?

He shook his head to dispel the ridiculous thought. Aside from the fact that neither of them was looking for anything beyond some no-strings fun, he was hesitant to start anything long-term with any woman. His father had been the most honorable man he had ever known and from what he remembered and everything everyone said, Charles Lassiter had loved his wife with all his heart. If his father couldn't remain faithful, what made Chance think that he could do any better?

"Uncle Chance, Fee said we could play fashion show with my dolls the next time she's at Grandma Marlene's house," Cassie said, tugging on his shirtsleeve. "When will that be?"

He'd been so preoccupied with his unsettling thoughts that he hadn't even noticed Fee and Cassie had returned. "I'll talk to Grandma Marlene and see what we can work out," he said, smiling as he picked Cassie up to sit on his forearm. "How does that sound, princess?"

Yawning, Cassie nodded. "Good."

"I think someone is getting sleepy," Fee said when

Chance opened the rear passenger door and buckled Cassie into her safety seat.

"She'll be asleep before we get out of the parking lot," he said, closing the door and turning to help Fee into the truck.

When he got in behind the steering wheel and started the engine, Fee smiled. "After she goes to sleep, we'll have some time to talk."

"About the campaign?" he guessed, steering the truck out onto the road.

"I'd like to hear what your main objections are to being the spokesman," she said, settling back in the bucket seat.

"Being the center of attention isn't something I'm comfortable with and never have been," he said honestly.

"But it would only be some still photos and a few videos," she insisted. "We could even cut out the few personal appearances unless you decided you wanted to do them."

"Yeah, those are out of the question," he said firmly. As far as he was concerned those appearances she mentioned had been off the table from the get-go. "Like I told you the other day at lunch, I don't intend to be a monkey in a sideshow. What you see with me is what you get, sweetheart. I wouldn't know how to be an actor if I tried."

"What if we filmed the video spots on the ranch?" she asked, sounding as if she was thinking out loud. "I could have a cameraman take some footage of you riding up on your horse and then all you would have to do is read from a cue card." She paused for a moment. "We could probably even lift still shots from that."

He could tell she wasn't going to give up. "I'm by no means making any promises," he said, wondering what he could say that would discourage her. "But I'll have to think a little more about it."

"Okay," she said slowly. He could tell she wasn't happy that she hadn't wrangled an agreement from him.

Reaching over, he covered her hand with his. "I'm not saying no, Fee. I'm just saying I need more time to think it over."

When she looked at him, her expression hopeful, he almost caved in and told her he would be her spokesman. Fortunately, she didn't give him the opportunity.

"That's fair," she said, suddenly grinning. "But just keep in mind, I'm not giving up."

"It never occurred to me that you would," he said, laughing.

Fee sat in the middle of the bed with her laptop and an array of papers spread out around her on the colorful quilt. She was supposed to be working on the Lassiter PR campaign. But in the past hour, she had found herself daydreaming about a tall, handsome, green-eyed cowboy more than she had been thinking about ways to restore the public's faith in his family.

Watching him interact with his niece that afternoon had been almost as eye-opening as witnessing his skill at helping a cow give birth to her calf. Both times she had seen him interact with his niece, he had listened patiently when the child spoke and always made Cassie feel as if everything she said was of the utmost importance to him. Someday Chance was going to be a wonderful father and Fee couldn't help but feel a twinge of envy for the woman who would bear his child.

Her heart skipped a beat and she shook her head to dispel the unwarranted thought. What was wrong with her? Why was she even thinking about Chance having a child with some unknown woman?

It shouldn't matter to her. By the end of her month's stay, she would be back in Los Angeles scheduling commercial spots for the family campaign and working toward her goal of becoming Lassiter Media's first female public relations vice president under the age of thirty. And unlike being in Wyoming, she would enjoy the convenience of not having to drive forty miles just to reach a town where she could shop or dine out.

But as she sat there thinking about her life back in L.A., she couldn't seem to remember what the appeal of living there had been. Her condo building was filled with people she didn't know and didn't care to know. And for reasons she couldn't put her finger on, the job promotion didn't seem nearly as enticing as it had a week ago.

As she sat there trying to figure out why she was feeling less than enthusiastic about her life in California, there was a knock on her closed door. Gathering the papers around her to put back in the file folder, she turned off her laptop and walked over to find Chance standing on the other side of the door.

"It's a clear night and the moon is almost full," Chance said, leaning one shoulder against the door frame. "How would you like to go for a ride?"

"On a horse? Surely you can't be serious." She laughed as she shook her head. "I'm not that experienced at riding during the day. What makes you think I would be any better at night? Besides, don't wild animals prowl around more in the dark? There's probably something out there with sharp teeth and long claws just waiting for me to come riding along."

"Slow down, sweetheart. You're sounding a lot like Cassie," he said, laughing. "We won't be going far and other than a raccoon or a coyote, I doubt that we'll see any wildlife. Besides, you won't be riding Rosy. You'll be on the back of Dakota with me."

She gave him a doubtful look. "And you think that's an even better idea than me riding Rosy?"

He grinned as he rocked back on his heels. "Yup."

"I'll bet you even have a cozy little saddle made for two stashed in the tack room," she quipped.

"You're so cute." Laughing, he straightened to his full height and took her by the hand to lead her downstairs. "No, they don't make saddles for two people. We're going to ride bareback."

"Oh, yeah, that's even safer than me riding Rosy at night," she muttered as they left the house and started toward the barn.

"It is if you're a skilled horseman and you know your horse."

"Just remember, I'm counting on you to be right about that," she said, unable to believe she was going along with his scheme.

When they reached the barn, he led Dakota out of his stall and put a bridle on the gelding. Then turning, he loosely put his arms around her. "Thanks for going with me and Cassie today," he said, kissing her temple. "I know she enjoyed talking to you about her dolls."

"She's a delightful little girl. Very bright and outgoing," Fee said. "I had a wonderful time talking to her." Grinning, she added, "But I'm really surprised that you didn't join in the conversation when we were discussing the latest doll accessories."

"I'll be the first to admit I don't know diddly-squat about dolls." He chuckled. "But if you want to talk toy trucks or action figures, I'm you're guy."

"I'll take your word for that, too," she said, staring up into his eyes. "But all joking aside, I really did have fun chatting with your niece."

"What about me?" he whispered, leaning forward. "Did you have a good time talking with me?"

A quivering excitement ran through her body at the feel of his warm breath feathering over her ear and she had to brace her hands on his biceps to keep her balance. The feel of rock-hard muscle beneath his chambray shirt caused heat to flow through her veins.

"Yes, I always enjoy talking to you," she answered truthfully.

"I like spending my time with you, too." Lowering his head, he gave her a kiss so tender her knees threatened to buckle before he stepped back, took hold of the reins and a handful of Dakota's mane, then swung up onto the horse. "Turn your back to me, Fee."

When she did as he instructed, he reached down and effortlessly lifted her to sit in front of him on the gelding. Straddling the horse, she was glad Chance was holding on to her. "Whoa! This is a lot higher than sitting on Rosy."

Chance's deep chuckle vibrated against her back as he tightened his arm around her midsection and nudged the gelding into a slow walk. "I promise you're safe, sweetheart. I won't let you fall."

She knew he was talking about a fall from the horse, but what was going to keep her from falling for the man holding her so securely against him?

Fee quickly relegated the thought to the back of her mind as Dakota carried them from the barn out into the night and she gazed up at the sky. Billions of stars created a twinkling canopy above and the moon cast an ethereal glow over the rugged landscape.

"This is gorgeous, Chance." She shook her head. "I've never seen so many stars in the night sky before."

"That's because of smog and too many lights in the city to see them all," he answered, his voice low and intimate. He tightened his arms around her. "Are you chilly?"

She could lie and tell him that she was, but she suspected that he already knew her tiny shiver was caused by their close proximity. "Not really," she admitted, leaning her head back against his shoulder. "It's just that something this vast and beautiful is humbling."

They rode along in silence for some time before she felt the evidence of his reaction to being this close to her against her backside. So overwhelmed by the splendor of the night, she hadn't paid attention to the fact that her bottom was nestled tightly between his thighs. But it wasn't his arousal that surprised her as much as her reaction to it. Knowing that he desired her caused an answering warmth to spread throughout her body and an empty ache to settle in the most feminine part of her.

"Chance?"

"Don't freak out," he whispered, stopping Dakota. "I'm not going to deny that I want you. You're a desirable woman and I'm like any other man—I have needs. But nothing is going to happen unless it's what you want, too, sweetheart."

Before she could find her voice, Chance released his hold on her and slid off the horse to his feet. He immediately reached up to help her down, then wrapping his arms around her, gave her a kiss that caused her toes to curl inside her boots before he set her away from him.

Disappointed that the kiss had been so brief, she

tried to distract herself by looking around. Something shiny caught her attention and taking a few steps closer, she realized it was the moon reflecting off of a small pool of water. Surrounded on three sides by cottonwood trees, she could see wisps of mist rising from its surface and the faint sound of running water.

"Is that a natural spring?" she asked.

"It's actually considered a thermal spring even though the temperature never gets over about seventy-five degrees," Chance said, walking over to stand beside her. "I used to go swimming in it when I was a kid."

"It's that deep?" she asked, intrigued. Even with just the light from the moon, she could see a shadowy image of the bottom of the pool.

"It's only about four feet deep over by the outlet where it runs down to the river." He laughed. "But to a ten-year-old kid that's deep enough to get in and splash around."

Fee smiled as she thought of Chance playing in the water as a child. "I'm sure you had a lot of fun. I used to love going to the beach when I was young, and my grandmother's house had a swimming pool."

"We always had a pool up at the main house," he said, nodding. "But it's not as much fun as this. Have you ever been skinny-dipping?" he asked.

"No." She laughed. "Besides not really having the nerve to do it, I would have hated causing Mr. Harris next door to have a coronary, or scandalizing his wife to the point where she refused to go to the senior center with my grandmother to play bingo."

He gave her a wicked grin and reached down to pull off his boots and socks. "I will if you will."

"Skinny-dip? Here? Now?" She shook her head. "Have you lost your mind? Aren't you worried someone will see you?"

He tugged his shirt from his jeans and with one smooth motion released all of the snap closures. "Sweetheart, it's just you, me and Dakota out here. And since he's a gelding, all he's interested in is grass."

She glanced over at the horse. "What if he runs away and leaves us stranded out here?"

"He's trained to ground tie." He reached to unbuckle his belt and release the button at the top of his jeans. "As long as the ends of the reins are dragging the ground, he'll stay close." His grin widened. "Are you going to join me?"

"I don't think so." She wasn't a prude, but she wasn't sure she was ready to abandon years of her grandmother's lectures on modesty, either.

"Now who isn't being adventurous?" he teased.

"Trying a different flavor of ice cream is completely different than taking off all of your..." Her voice trailed off when Chance shrugged out of his shirt.

The man had the physique of a male model and she had firsthand knowledge of how hard and strong all those muscles were. She thought about how every time he helped her into his truck or lifted her onto one of the horses, he picked her up as if she weighed nothing.

Unable to look away when he unzipped his fly and shoved his jeans down his long muscular legs, Fee felt a lazy heat begin to flow through her veins. "I can't believe you're really going to do this."

"Yup, I'm really going to do this," he repeated as he stepped out of his jeans and tossed them on top of his shirt. When she continued to stare at him, he grinned as he hooked his thumbs into the waistband of his boxer briefs. "I'm not the least bit shy and don't mind you watching one little bit, but unless you want to see me in my birthday suit, you might want to close your eyes now."

"Oh!" She spun around. "Let me know when you're in the water."

"All clear," he announced. When she turned back, Chance was standing up in the pool. The water barely covered his navel. "You really should join me. The water is the perfect temperature."

"I can't," she said, shaking her head as she avoided looking below his bare chest. "It isn't deep enough."

"You know you want to," he said, grinning.

She didn't believe for a minute that he would keep his eyes averted as she was doing, but he was right about one thing. She was tempted to throw caution to the wind and go skinny-dipping for the first time in her life.

"I don't have a towel to dry off with." Her statement sounded lame even to her.

"We can dry off with my shirt," he offered.

"And you promise not to look?" she asked, knowing that his answer and what he would actually do were probably two different things.

"Scout's honor I won't look while you undress and get into the water," he said, raising his hand in a three-finger oath.

"Then close your eyes," she said decisively as she reached to pull the tail of her T-shirt from her jeans.

When he did, she quickly removed her boots and socks, then stripped out of her clothing before she had a chance to change her mind. Stepping into the water, she immediately covered her breasts with her arms and bent her knees until the water came up to her neck.

"I can't believe I'm actually doing this," she said between nervous giggles.

"Look at it this way," he said, opening his eyes. His low, intimate tone and the look on his handsome face as he moved through the water toward her made Fee feel as if he had cast a spell over her. "It's something you can check off your bucket list."

"I don't have a list," she said slowly.

"I'll help you make one." His gaze held hers as he reached beneath the water and lifted her to her feet. Taking her into his arms, he smiled. "Then I'll help you check off all of the new things you're doing."

Her arms automatically rose to encircle his neck and the moment her wet breasts pressed against his wide, bare chest a jolt of excitement rocked her. "You said you wouldn't look."

"I haven't…yet." His slow smile caused a nervous

energy in the deepest part of her. "But I never said I wouldn't touch you."

As he lowered his head, Fee welcomed the feel of his firm mouth covering hers. Chance's kisses were drugging and quickly becoming an addiction that she wasn't certain she could ever overcome.

The thought should have sent her running as fast as she could to the Cheyenne airport and the earliest flight back to L.A. But as his lips moved over hers with such tenderness, she forgot all the reasons she shouldn't become involved with him or any other man. All she could think about was the way he made her feel.

When he coaxed her to open for him, she couldn't have denied him if her life depended on it. At the first touch of his tongue to hers, it felt as if an electric current danced over every one of her nerve endings and a tiny moan escaped her parted lips. She wanted him, wanted to feel his arms around her and the strength of his lovemaking in every fiber of her being.

The feel of his hard arousal against her lower belly was proof he wanted her just as badly. The realization created a restlessness within her and she was so lost in the myriad sensations Chance had created, it took her a moment to realize he was ending the kiss.

"As bad as I hate to say this, I think we'd better head back to the house." His voice sounded a lot like a rusty hinge. "I have a good idea where this is headed and I don't have protection for us."

Covering her breasts with her arms, she nodded

reluctantly. There was no way she could deny that the passion between them was heading in that direction. Thank goodness he had the presence of mind to call a halt to it.

"Turn around."

He laughed. "Really? Our nude bodies were just pressed together from head to toe and you're worried about me seeing you?"

Her cheeks heated. "Feeling is one thing, seeing is entirely different."

"If you say so," he said, doing as she requested.

Hurriedly getting out of the water, Fee turned her back to him, used his shirt to quickly dry herself and then pulled on her panties and jeans. But when she searched for her bra, she couldn't seem to find it anywhere.

"Looking for this?" Chance asked.

Glancing over her shoulder, he was standing right behind her with her bra hanging from his index finger like a limp flag. "I thought you were supposed to stay in the water with your back turned until I got dressed," she scolded, taking her lacy brassiere from him to put the garment on.

"I stayed in the water right up until you started searching for your bra." She heard him pulling on his clothes. "After you dried off, you dropped my shirt on it when you reached for your panties."

"You watched me get dressed? You swore you wouldn't peek."

"Yeah, about that." He turned her to face him and the slow smile curving his mouth caused her to catch her breath. "I was never a Scout so that oath earlier didn't really count. But just for the record, I told you before I kissed you that I hadn't looked *yet*. I didn't say I wasn't going to." He gave her a quick kiss, then bent to pull on his socks and boots.

While he walked over to where Dakota stood munching on a patch of grass, Fee picked up his damp shirt and waited for him to help her onto the gelding's back. She should probably call her boss at Lassiter Media and arrange for someone else to take over the PR campaign, then head back to L.A. to get her priorities straight before she committed career suicide. But she rejected that idea immediately. No matter how difficult the assignment, she had never bowed out of a project and she wasn't going to back down now.

She was just going to have to be stronger and resist the temptation of Chance Lassiter. But heaven help her, she had a feeling it was going to be the hardest thing she'd ever have to do.

Chance lay in bed and damned his sense of responsibility for at least the hundredth time since he and Fee had returned to the house. He hadn't taken her on the moonlight ride with the intention of seducing her. On the contrary, it had simply been something he thought she might enjoy and he'd been right. She'd loved seeing all the billions of stars twinkling in the night sky.

At least, that's the way things had started out. What he hadn't allowed himself to consider was the effect her body would have on his when they rode double. Her delightful little bottom rubbing against the most vulnerable part of him had quickly proven to be the greatest test of his fortitude he'd ever faced. Then, if he hadn't been insane enough, she'd noticed the spring and he'd had the brilliant idea of going skinny-dipping.

"Yeah, like that didn't have disaster written all over it," he muttered as he stared up at the ceiling.

If he'd just stayed on his side of the pool and hadn't touched her or kissed her, he wouldn't be lying there feeling as if he was ready to climb the walls. But the allure of her being so close had been more than he could fight and once he'd touched her, he couldn't have stopped himself from kissing her any more than he could get Gus to give up baseball.

But what had really sent him into orbit had been her response. The minute their lips met, Fee had melted against him and his body had hardened so fast it had left him feeling as if he might pass out. The feel of her breasts against his chest and his arousal pressing into her soft lower belly had damn near driven him over the edge and he'd come dangerously close to forgetting about their protection.

Fortunately, he'd had enough strength left to be responsible. But that hadn't been easy.

He punched his pillow and turned to his side. No two ways around it, he should have known better. But he'd been fool enough to think that he could control the situation and ended up being the victim of his own damned arrogance.

He'd known full well the moment he'd laid eyes on her at Hannah and Logan's wedding, a spark ignited within him and with each day since the fire had increased to the point it was about to burn him up from the inside out. He wanted her, wanted to sink himself so deeply within her velvet depths that neither of them could remember where he ended and she began. And unless he was reading her wrong, it was what she wanted, too. So why was he in bed on one side of the hall and she in bed on the other now?

With a guttural curse that his mother would have had a fit over, Chance threw back the sheet and sat up on the side of the bed. Two hours of tossing and turning had gotten him nowhere. Maybe a drink would help him calm down enough to get a few hours of sleep.

Pulling on a pair of jeans, he didn't bother with a shirt as he left the master suite and stared at the closed door across the hall. He'd like nothing better than to go into that room, pick Fee up and carry her back to his bed. Instead, he forced himself to turn and walk barefoot down the hall to the stairs.

When he reached the kitchen, he went straight to the refrigerator for a beer, and then walked out onto the back porch. Hopefully, the beer and the cool night air would work their magic and help him relax.

Chance took a long draw from the bottle in his hand and stared out into the night as he tried to forget about the desirable woman upstairs. He needed to make a trip into town tomorrow for some supplies, as well as to stop by Lassiter Media's Cheyenne office to pick up his tickets for Frontier Days at the end of the month. Because Lassiter donated the use of some of their audio and video equipment for the annual event, the rodeo organizers always gave the company complimentary tickets. He attended the finals of the event every year and he thought Fee might enjoy going with him, even if she was back at the rental house by then.

Lightning streaked across the western sky, followed by the distant sound of thunder. It appeared the weather was as unsettled as he was, he thought as he downed the rest of his beer and headed back inside.

As he climbed the stairs a flash of lightning briefly illuminated his way and by the time he started down the upstairs hall, a trailing clap of thunder loud enough to wake the dead rattled the windows and reverberated throughout the house. He had just reached the master suite when the door to Fee's room flew open. When she came rushing out, she ran headlong into him.

"Whoa there, sweetheart." He placed his hands on her shoulders to keep her from falling backward. "What's wrong?"

"What was that noise?" she asked breathlessly.

"It's getting ready to storm," he said, trying his best not to notice how her sweet scent seemed to swirl around him and the fact that she had on a silky red nightgown that barely covered her panties.

"It sounded like an explosion," she said, seeming as if she might be a little disoriented.

"It's just a little thunder." He should probably be

ashamed of himself, but he had never been more thankful for a thunderstorm in his life. "You have storms in L.A., don't you?"

Nodding, she jumped when another clap of thunder resounded around them. "Not that many. And I never liked them when we did."

Chance put his arms around her and tried to remind himself that he was offering her comfort. "I guess I'm more used to them because at this time of year we have one almost every day."

"Really? That many?" She was beginning to sound more awake.

He nodded. "Occasionally we'll have severe storms, but most of the them are a lot like Gus—more noise than anything else."

"I think I'm glad I live in L.A. The city noise masks some of the thunder," she said, snuggling against his bare chest. "I'd be a nervous wreck if I lived here."

Chance felt a little let down. He wanted her to love the Big Blue ranch as much as he did even if she was only in Wyoming for a short time. But it wasn't as if he had been hoping she would relocate to the area. All he wanted was a summer fling.

Right now, he didn't have the presence of mind to give his unwarranted disappointment a lot of thought. Fee was clinging to him as if he was her lifeline and her scantily clad body pressed to his wasn't helping his earlier restlessness one damn bit. In fact, it was playing hell with his good intentions, causing his body to react in a way that she probably wouldn't appreciate, considering the situation.

"I'm going to drive into Cheyenne tomorrow to pick up some supplies and rodeo tickets," he said in an effort to distract both of them. "I thought we could have lunch at Lassiter Grill. Dylan and Jenna are back from their honeymoon and I figured you might like to see them."

"I'd like that very much." Her long blond hair brushed against his chest when she nodded. "Jenna and I became pretty good friends when I worked on the ads for the grand opening," she added, oblivious to his turmoil. "I also helped her out when one of the reporters became obsessed with her at the opening of Lassiter Grill and started asking questions about her and her father."

Sage had told him about Jenna's father being a con artist and that the man had made it look as if she'd been in on one of his schemes. He'd also mentioned the incident with the reporter at the restaurant's opening and how effectively Fee had handled the situation.

"Then that's what we'll do," he said, finding it harder with each passing second to ignore the heat building in his groin.

Another crash of thunder caused Fee to burrow even closer and Chance gave up trying to be noble. He had reached his limit and he was man enough to admit it.

"Fee?"

When she raised her head, he lowered his and

gave in to temptation, consequences be damned. It wasn't as if he'd been able to sleep anyway. He was going to give her a kiss that was guaranteed to keep them both up for the rest of the night.

Six

When Chance brought his mouth down on hers, Fee forgot all about her vow to be strong and try to resist him. The truth was, she wanted his kiss, wanted to once again experience the way only he could make her feel.

As his lips moved over hers, a calming warmth began to spread throughout her body, and she knew without question that as long as she was in his arms she would always be safe. But she didn't have time to think about what her insight might mean before he coaxed her with his tongue.

When his arms tightened around her and he deepened the kiss, she felt as if her bones had turned to rubber. The taste of need on his firm male lips, the feel of his solid bare chest pressed against her breasts and the hard ridge of his arousal cushioned by her stomach sent ribbons of desire threading their way through her.

He brought his hand around from her back up along her ribs. When he cupped her breast, then worried the taut peak with his thumb, her silk nightie chafing the sensitive nub felt absolutely wonderful and she closed her eyes to savor the sensation.

"I know all you want from me right now is reassurance," he said, nibbling kisses from her lips down the column of her neck to her collarbone. "But I've wanted you from the moment I first saw you at my sister's wedding." He left a trail of kisses from her chest to the V neckline of her short nightgown before pulling away. "If that's not what you want, too, then now would be the time for you to go back into your room and close the door."

Opening her eyes, she saw the passion reflected in his and it thrilled her. Fee knew what she should do. She should return to her room, pack her things and have him take her back to the corporate rental house in Cheyenne the first thing tomorrow morning. But that wasn't what she was going to do. It could very well prove to be the biggest mistake she'd ever made, but she wasn't going to think about her job or the danger of doing something foolish that could cause her to lose it.

"Chance, I don't want to go back to my room," she said, realizing she really didn't have a choice in the matter. They had been heading toward this moment since she looked up and watched him escort the matron of honor back up the aisle at his sister's wedding.

He closed his eyes and took a long, deep breath before he opened them again and gazed down at her. "I'm not looking for anything long-term, Fee."

"Neither am I," she said truthfully.

She ignored the little twinge of sadness that accompanied her agreement. She wasn't interested in anything beyond her time in Wyoming. At the end of her stay, she would go back to her life in California and he would stay here on the Big Blue ranch. Other than a trip back to film the video for the Lassiter PR campaign, they wouldn't be seeing each other again. That's the way it was supposed to be—the way it had to be.

"Let's go into my room, sweetheart," he said, taking her by the hand to lead her across the hall to the master suite.

The lightning flashed and thunder continued to rumble loudly outside, but Fee barely noticed as Chance closed the door behind them and led her over to the side of his king-size bed. When he turned on the bedside lamp, she looked around. The furniture was made of rustic logs, and with the exception of a silver picture frame sitting on the dresser, the room was decorated in the same Western theme as the rest of the house. The photo inside was of a young boy and a man who looked a lot like Chance. Before she could ask if it was a picture of him and his father, Chance caught her to him for a kiss that sent waves of heat coursing through her and made her forget everything but the man holding her.

"Do you have any idea how many times I've thought about doing this over the past week?" he asked as he ran his index finger along the thin strap of her nightie. "Every time I've looked at you, it's all I can think about."

"I hadn't…really given it…a lot of thought." Did he expect her to form a coherent answer when the intimate tone of his voice and his passionate words were sending shivers of anticipation through every part of her?

Needing to touch him, she placed her palms on his chest. "I have, however, thought a lot about you and how much I've wanted to do this." She ran her fingertips over the thick pads of his pectoral muscles and a heady sense of feminine power came over her when she felt a shudder run through him. "Your body is perfect. I thought so when we were at the spring." She touched one flat male nipple. "I wanted to touch you then, but—"

"By the time the night is over, I intend for both of us to know each other's body as well as we know our own," he said, sliding his hands down her sides to the lace hem of her nightgown.

His sensuous smile caused an interesting little tingle deep inside her as he lifted the garment up and over her head, and then tossed it aside. He caught her hands in his, took a step back and held her arms wide. His eyes seemed to caress her, the need she detected in their green depths stealing her breath.

"You're absolutely beautiful, Fee."

"So are you, Chance."

He gave her a smile that curled her toes, then brought her hands back up to his broad chest. "Ladies first."

She realized that he wanted her to feel comfortable with him and was willing to allow her to explore him before he touched her. His concession caused emotion to clog her throat. She'd never known any man as thoughtful and unselfish as Chance Lassiter.

Enjoying the feel of his warm bare flesh beneath her palms, she ran her hands down his chest to the ripples of muscle below. When she reached his navel, she quickly glanced up. His eyes were closed and his head was slightly tilted back as if he struggled for control.

"Does that feel good?" she asked, kissing his smooth skin as she trailed her finger down the thin line of dark hair from his navel to where it disappeared into the waistband of his jeans.

"Sweetheart, if it felt any better, I'm not sure I could handle it," he said, sounding as if he'd run a marathon. When she opened the snap, he stopped her and took a step back. "I don't want you to get the wrong idea. I'd love nothing more than to have you take my jeans off me, but this time it's something I have to take care of myself."

Slightly confused, she watched him ease the zipper down and when his fly gaped open, she realized the reason for his concern. "If I had tried… Oh, my… That could have been disastrous."

Grinning, he nodded as he shoved his jeans down

his long, heavily muscled legs and kicked them over to join her nightgown where it lay on the floor. "When I got up to go get a drink, I just grabbed a pair of jeans. I didn't bother putting on underwear."

Fee had purposely kept her eyes above his waist in the pool, but as she gazed at him now, she realized how truly magnificent his body was. Chance's shoulders were impossibly wide, his chest and abdomen sculpted with muscles made hard from years of ranch work. As her gaze drifted lower, she caught her breath. She'd felt his arousal when they'd gone skinny-dipping, but the strength of his desire for her was almost overwhelming.

"Don't ever doubt that I want you, Fee," he said, taking her into his arms. He lowered his head to softly kiss her lips, then nibbled his way down to the slope of her breast. "You're the most desirable woman I've ever met."

Her pulse raced as he slowly kissed his way to the hardened peak. But the moment he took the tip into his mouth, it felt as if her heart stopped and time stood still. Never in her entire twenty-nine years had she experienced anything as exquisite or electrifying as the feel of Chance's soft kiss on her rapidly heating body. When he turned his attention to her other breast, her head fell back and she found it hard to draw in enough air.

"Does that feel good?" he asked.

Unable to speak, she merely nodded.

Taking a step back, he held her gaze with his as he hooked his thumbs in the waistband of her bikini panties and slowly pulled them down her legs. When they fell to her ankles and she stepped out of them, he smiled and wrapped his arms around her. The feel of her softer skin pressed to his hard flesh caused her to sag against him.

He swung her up into his arms to carefully place her on the bed and she didn't think she'd ever felt more cherished. She watched him reach into the bedside table to remove a foil packet, then tucking it under his pillow, Chance stretched out on the bed beside her. He'd no sooner taken her back into his arms when lightning flashed outside and a loud clap of thunder caused the windows to rattle.

When the lamp flickered several times, he gathered her to him. "It looks like we might lose power."

The feel of all of him against her caused a shiver of excitement to course through her. "I'd forgotten it was even storming."

"And I intend to make sure you forget about it again," he said, covering her mouth with his.

He kissed her tenderly and ran his hand along her side to her hip. The light abrasion of his calloused palm as he leisurely caressed her was breathtaking, but when he moved his hand to touch her intimately, Fee wasn't certain she would ever breathe again.

As he stroked her with a feathery touch, the ache of unfulfilled desire coiled inside her. She needed him more than she'd ever needed anything in her life, but she wanted to touch him—to learn about him the same as he was learning about her.

When she moved her hands from his chest and

found him, he went completely still a moment before he groaned. "You're going to ruin…all my… good intentions, Fee."

"What would those be?" she asked as she measured his length and girth with her palms.

"I'd like to make this first time last…a little longer than what it's going to…if you keep doing that," he said, taking her hands to place them back on his chest. He took several deep breaths, then reached beneath his pillow. "I want you so much, I'd rather not finish the race before you get to the starting gate, sweetheart."

When he arranged their protection, he took her back into his arms and kissed her as he nudged her knees apart. Then capturing her gaze with his, he gave her a smile that sent heat coursing through her veins. "Show me where you want me, Fee."

Without a moment's hesitation, she guided him to her and he joined their bodies in one smooth thrust. He went perfectly still for a moment and she knew he was not only giving her time to adjust to being filled completely by him, he was also struggling to gain control.

"You're so beautiful and perfect," he finally said as he slowly began to rock against her.

"So are you," she managed as her body began to move in unison with his.

Fee felt as if she had been custom-made just for him and as Chance increased the rhythm of his thrusts, she became lost in the delicious sensations of their lovemaking. Heat filled her as she started climbing toward the fulfillment they both sought.

Unable to prolong the inevitable, she reluctantly gave herself up to the tension building within her. As waves of pleasure coursed through every cell in her being, she clung to him to keep from being lost. A moment later, she felt his body stiffen and knew he'd found his own satisfaction.

Wrapping her arms around his shoulders when he collapsed on top of her, Fee held him tight. She had never felt closer to anyone in her entire life than she did to Chance at that moment and she didn't want the connection to end.

The thought that she might be falling for him crossed her mind and caused her a moment's panic, but she gave herself a mental shake. It was true that she cared for him more than she could remember caring for any man, but that didn't mean she was falling in love with him. Chance was intelligent, caring and the most selfless man she'd ever met, and any woman would be lucky to win his heart. But she wasn't that woman.

The next morning as Chance got dressed, he smiled at the woman curled up in his bed. Fee was sound asleep and he wasn't going to wake her. They had spent most of the night making love and she had to be every bit as tired as he was. But he had chores to do and a ranch to run. Otherwise, he'd crawl back in bed, make love to her again and then hold her while they both slept.

As he stepped out into the hall, he regretfully closed the door behind him. He had never met any woman who felt as good or as natural in his arms as Fee did. She was amazing in just about every way he could think of, and even though she was a good nine or ten inches shorter than his six-foot-one-inch frame, when they made love they fit together perfectly.

Yawning as he entered the kitchen, he smiled when he thought about why he was so tired. "Gus, Fee and I are going into Cheyenne later this morning," he said, walking straight to the coffeemaker to pour himself a cup of the strong brew. "Is there anything you need me to pick up while I'm there?"

"Can't think of a thing," Gus said, opening the oven. "Where's Fee?"

"The storm kept her awake most of the night," Chance answered, going over to sit down at the table. "I thought I'd let her sleep in this morning."

When Gus turned, he stared at Chance for several long seconds before he slammed the pan of biscuits he had just removed from the oven onto the butcher-block island. "What the hell are you thinkin', boy?"

"What do you mean?" He was used to Gus and his off-the-wall questions and normally managed to figure out what the old man was talking about. But Chance had no idea what he'd done to piss the old boy off this early in the morning.

"I wasn't born yesterday," Gus said, shaking his head. "That storm moved on just past midnight and if you hadn't been awake with her, how would you know she didn't sleep?"

With his coffee cup halfway to his mouth, Chance stopped to glare at his old friend, then slowly set it down on the table. "Watch it, Gus. You're about to head into territory that isn't any of your concern."

"That little gal up in your bed ain't the kind of woman you bed, unless you're willin' to change her name," Gus said, ignoring Chance's warning.

"When did you become an expert on the subject of women?" Chance asked, doing his best to hold his anger in check out of respect for Gus's age and the fact that he was more like family than an employee.

"I never said I was an expert." Gus walked over to shake his finger at Chance. "But there's women you have a good time with and the kind you court for a while and marry." He pointed his index finger up at the ceiling. "That little gal upstairs is the courtin' kind."

"She's not interested in getting serious any more than I am," Chance said defensively.

"That may be what she's sayin'," Gus insisted. "And she probably even believes it. But I've heard how she goes on about you and the look in her eyes when you walk in a room." He grunted. "Your momma wore the same look every time she looked at your daddy."

"Yeah and we both know how that turned out," Chance muttered.

"Boy, don't go judgin' a man till you walk a mile

in his boots," Gus advised. "Your daddy loved your momma more than life itself."

"Is that why I've got a half sister from the affair he had with Hannah's mother?" Chance shot back before he could stop himself. He loved that he finally had a sibling, but the truth of the matter was, Charles Lassiter had cheated on his wife and that was something Chance wasn't sure he could ever come to terms with.

"Your daddy made a mistake and till the day he died, he did everything he could to make it up to your momma." Gus shook his head. "She forgave him, but I don't think he ever did forgive himself."

"Well, that's something I'll never have to deal with," Chance said, shrugging. "You can't cheat on your wife if you never get married."

Gus stared at him for a moment before he sighed heavily. "I never took you for a coward, boy."

Before Chance could tell Gus to mind his own damn business, he heard Fee coming down the stairs. "We'll finish this later."

"There ain't nothin' to finish," Gus said stubbornly. "I've said all I'm gonna say about it."

"Chance, why didn't you wake me?" Fee asked, entering the kitchen. "I wanted to help you feed Belle and her mother this morning."

"I thought I'd let you sleep in." Rising to his feet, Chance walked over and got a cup from the cupboard to pour her some coffee instead of taking her into his arms and kissing her the way he wanted to. "I know the storm kept you up last night and thought you could use the sleep." When Gus coughed, he glared at the old fart a moment before he walked over to set her coffee on the table. "I'll go out to the barn and give Slim the list of things I want him and the boys to get done today. Then after breakfast we'll feed the cow and calf before we take off to go into Cheyenne."

Her smile sent his hormones racing. "Great! I'll help Gus finish breakfast while you go talk to your foreman."

As Chance walked out of the house and across the yard, he thought about what Gus had said and how irritated he'd been with the old guy. Gus had been best friends with Charles Lassiter for years and it was only natural that he would defend him. And Chance had to admit that being out on the rodeo circuit had probably been lonely for his father without his family with him. But as far as Chance was concerned there was no excuse for infidelity. When a man committed himself to a woman, he didn't go looking for relief in another woman's arms.

That's why Chance had made the decision to remain single. Finding out a couple of months ago that a man like his father hadn't been able to resist temptation was enough to make Chance question a lot of things about himself. With the exception of his college girlfriend, he'd never been in a relationship for any real length of time. He'd always thought that was because he hadn't met the right woman. But could it be a clue he was incapable of committing himself to one woman? He wasn't sure and until he knew the answer to that question, his best bet would be to avoid getting too deeply involved with anyone. He certainly didn't want to run the risk of causing any woman the emotional pain that he was certain his mother had gone through.

He shook his head as he walked into the barn. He didn't know why he was giving anything Gus said a second thought. Gus had never been married and to Chance's knowledge the old guy hadn't had a date in more than twenty-five years. That wasn't exactly a glowing recommendation for Gus's advice on matters of the heart.

Besides, there were too many differences between Chance and Fee for anything to work out between them. She was a city girl who loved spending a day at the spa or in a boutique on Rodeo Drive, while he would rather go skinny-dipping or attend a rodeo. And then there was the matter of their jobs. She had a nice clean office in a climate-controlled skyscraper in downtown L.A. and his job required being out in all kinds of weather, doing things that most people considered dirty and thoroughly disgusting.

He took a deep breath and faced the facts. When Fee had to go back to L.A., he would tell her to get in touch with him whenever she was in town, kiss her goodbye and let her go. That was just the way it would have to be. But what he couldn't figure out was why the thought of her leaving made him feel completely empty inside.

"Chance is amazing with animals," Fee said to Jenna Montgomery-Lassiter after they enjoyed lunch at her new husband's restaurant. Chance and Dylan had gone into the office to discuss an increase in the amount of beef the Big Blue supplied to the Lassiter Grill chain, giving the women time for a little girl talk.

"Colleen and I have come to the conclusion that all of the Lassiter men are pretty amazing," Jenna agreed, grinning. "They aren't necessarily easy to love, but they are more than worth the effort."

"I'm sure they are," Fee said, smiling. "But I'm not in love with Chance."

Jenna gazed at her for several long moments. "Are you sure about that?"

Fee nodded. "We're just friends. I'm trying to talk him into helping me with the PR campaign to improve the Lassiter public image." Laughing, she added, "And he's trying to talk me out of it."

She felt a little guilty about not applying more pressure in her arguments to get him to agree to be the spokesman. But she sensed that the "hard sell" approach wouldn't work with him. If anything, it would make him that much more determined not to take on the job. And then there was the distraction he posed. Much of her time had been taken up with thinking about how soft his kisses were and how his touch made her feel as if she was the most cherished woman in the world.

"I'm sure Chance has been *very* persuasive," Jenna commented, her smile indicating that she knew something Fee didn't.

"What do you mean?" Fee couldn't imagine what her friend was alluding to.

Without answering, Jenna reached into her purse, handed Fee a small mirror, then tapped the side of her own neck with her index finger.

Looking into the mirror, Fee gasped and immediately pulled her long hair forward to hide the tiny blemish on the side of her neck. "I… Well, that is… We…" She clamped her mouth shut. There wasn't anything she could say. The little love bite on the side of her neck said it all.

To ease her embarrassment, Jenna smiled as she reached over to place a comforting hand on Fee's forearm. "It's barely noticeable and I probably would have missed it completely if I hadn't had one myself when we were on our honeymoon in Paris."

Her cheeks feeling as if they were on fire, Fee shook her head. "I haven't had one of those since I was a sophomore in college."

"The Lassiter men are very passionate," Jenna said, her tone reflecting her understanding. "It's one of the reasons we love them so much."

"I told you, Chance and I aren't in love," Fee insisted.

"I know," Jenna interrupted. "But I've seen the way you look at each other." She smiled. "If you two aren't there yet, it's just a matter of time."

Fee wasn't going to insult Jenna's intelligence by trying to deny that she was having to fight to keep herself from falling head over heels for Chance. "We're so different. I'm completely out of my element on the ranch, the same as he would be in a city the size of L.A."

"Differences are what makes things interesting," Jenna replied. "Heaven only knows, Dylan and I had our share. But if you really care deeply for someone, you work through the issues." She paused a moment. "I was certain that the implications of my father's illegal activities were going to tear Dylan and I apart. But we worked through that and our relationship is stronger than ever. If we can get past something like that, a little thing like distance between you and Chance should be a piece of cake to work out." She smiled. "You could always move here."

Fee stared down at her hands folded on top of the table for several seconds before she met Jenna's questioning gaze. "It's not just the distance of where we live that we'd have to work around," she said slowly. "I have a career that I won't give up." She sighed. "I won't bore you with the details, but my mother gave up a very promising career as a financial adviser because she fell in love with my father. After he left us, she'd been out of her field for so long, she decided it would be impossible to catch up." She shook her head. "I don't intend to give history the opportunity to repeat itself."

"I can understand wanting to maintain your independence," Jenna said, nodding. "But I don't think Chance would ever ask you to give up your career. He just doesn't impress me as being that type of man."

They both fell silent before Fee decided it was

time to lighten the mood. "Enough about that. Tell me about your honeymoon. I've never been to Paris. I've heard it's beautiful."

"It is," Jenna said, her eyes lighting up with enthusiasm. "Dylan spent a lot of time there when he was traveling through Europe and couldn't wait to show me all the little-known places he had discovered."

While her friend talked about the sites her husband had shown her in Paris, as well as the delectable French cuisine, Fee's thoughts strayed to Jenna's observations. If others could see how she felt about Chance, she probably was beginning to fall for him. He was a wonderful man and no matter how much she might deny it, she cared more deeply for him with each passing day and especially after making love last night.

But she couldn't allow herself to fall *in love* with Chance. Besides the fact that he had made it clear he wasn't looking for a relationship, she had far too much to lose. Not even taking into account the loss of her career, Fee could very easily end up facing a lifetime of heartache for a love that he could never return.

"Chance tells me you want him to be the family spokesman for the campaign," Dylan said, when he and Chance walked back to the table.

Fee nodded. "I believe he could be very convincing in getting the message across to the stockholders, as well as the public, that Lassiter Media is as solid as ever."

Dylan grinned as he and Chance took their seats. "I agree."

"Only because you're afraid she'll ask you to do it *if* I decide against it," Chance shot back.

"Well, there is that," Dylan said, laughing.

As she watched the two cousins' good-natured banter, Fee smiled. Of the three Lassiter men, she knew she had made the right choice. Chance wasn't as closed off as Sage and although Dylan was more open and outgoing than his brother, he had an air of sophistication about him that she didn't think would appeal to all demographics.

But she felt heartened by the exchange between Chance and Dylan. Chance hadn't said he wouldn't do the campaign; he had emphasized the word *if*. That had to mean he was considering the idea. Now all she had to do was get a firm commitment from Chance to be the family spokesman and she could start scheduling the video shoot.

A sadness began to fill her as she thought about what that meant. Once she had his agreement and the footage was filmed, she would go back to L.A. and he would stay on at the Big Blue. They might see each other occasionally at a Lassiter function, but eventually they would lose touch completely. Her chest tightened at the thought. No matter how many times she told herself that was the way it had to be, she knew it wasn't going to make their parting any easier. And she knew as surely as she knew her own name that she would be leaving her heart behind when she had to go.

Seven

Two days after their lunch with Dylan and Jenna, Chance watched Fee and his niece sitting cross-legged on the floor in the great room of the main ranch house having a good old time with Cassie's dolls. Fee was encouraging when the little girl wanted to try something different, listened attentively to everything Cassie said and wasn't the least bit put off by the child's constant questions.

No doubt about it, Fee was going to be a wonderful mother someday. The sudden thought that he wouldn't be the man giving her babies caused a knot to twist in his gut. Where had that come from? And why?

When he got up from the couch, Fee gave him a questioning look. "I think I'll go see if Mom needs help with dinner," he explained, thinking quickly. There was no way in hell he could tell her the real reason he was leaving the room.

"I should check to see if Marlene needs me to set the table," she said, starting to rise to her feet.

"No, you go ahead and have fun with your beauty pageant or fashion show or whatever it is you and Cassie are doing there," he said, forcing a laugh. "Mom loves to cook and probably already has everything under control. But I thought I'd offer just in case."

She smiled and the knot in his gut tightened painfully. "If I'm needed to do something, don't hesitate to come and tell me."

"I won't," he said, practically jogging from the room. The truth was, he needed to put some distance between them in order to come to terms with the fact that at some point in time another man was going to be holding her, loving her and raising a family with her. Up until two months ago when he learned about his father's failings, Chance had thought he'd have a shot at a family like that someday. Now he wasn't so sure that would ever happen.

Slowing his pace when he reached the hall, he walked into the kitchen, where his mother was getting ready to take a pot roast from the oven. If there was one thing Marlene Lassiter loved to do, it was cook, and even though the Lassiters could easily afford a world-class chef, she had always insisted on making the family meals herself. The only time he had ever known her to turn over the chore to someone else was when the ranch hosted a party or reception that required the hiring of a caterer.

"When are Hannah and Logan supposed to be back from the Caribbean?" he asked, walking over to take the pair of oven mitts from her. Opening the oven, he lifted the roast out and sat it on the counter for her. "I thought they were only going on a seven-day cruise."

"They got back from the cruise last night, but they are going to spend a few days in New Orleans seeing the sights before they fly back to Cheyenne," his mother said, smiling. He could tell that he and Fee had pleased her by accepting her dinner invitation when they'd brought Cassie back from her weekly trip for ice cream.

That only added a good dose of guilt to the feelings already twisting his gut. As he leaned against the counter and watched her arrange the roast on a platter with the potatoes and carrots around it, he decided there was no time like the present to get things out in the open and put them to rest once and for all. "Mom, I've been curious about something."

"What's that, dear?" she asked, turning to tear up lettuce for a salad.

"Why didn't you tell me about Hannah years ago instead of waiting until she showed up a couple of months back?" he asked point-blank.

He heard her soft gasp a moment before she stopped making the salad to turn and face him. "I know you feel cheated about not knowing you had a sister all these years, but it's the way it had to be, son. Hannah's mother didn't want her to know or have anything to do with the Lassiters. Whether I agreed with her decision or not, I respected those wishes because Hannah was her child, not mine."

"I know that's what you told me when we first met Hannah," Chance said slowly. "But why didn't she want Hannah to know about us?"

Marlene stared at him for a moment before she spoke. "I don't suppose it will hurt to tell you now." She sighed. "Ruth Lovell was a very bitter woman. She wanted your father to leave me and marry her. When he told her that wasn't going to happen, she refused to let Hannah have anything to do with any of us." She shook her head. "The ones who suffered the most from her decision were your father and Hannah. He didn't get to see his daughter more than a few times and she was too young to even know who he was."

"Did Dad ever try to get custody?" If he had been in his father's shoes, which he wouldn't have been in the first place, he'd have moved heaven and earth to be with his child.

Marlene nodded. "Your father consulted several lawyers, but back then a married man trying to gain custody of a child from an affair didn't have nearly the rights he has today."

Chance hesitated a moment, but since his mother brought up the subject of his father's affair, he was going to ask the question that had been bothering him since he learned about Hannah. "Why did you stay with him after he cheated on you with another woman? Weren't you angry and hurt by what he'd done?"

A faraway look entered his mother's eyes as if she might be looking back in time at the choices she'd made. "When Charles told me about his affair with Ruth Lovell, I was crushed," she admitted. "He was the love of my life and he'd betrayed me." She looked directly at Chance. "And don't think for a minute it was easy for me to stay with him or eventually forgive and start trusting him again. It wasn't. I struggled with that for quite some time before I accepted that your father had made a mistake he couldn't change, but one that he regretted with all of his heart."

"What finally convinced you to give him another chance?" he asked, still not fully comprehending her motivation to stay with a man who cheated on her.

"I finally realized that he was just as crushed by what he'd done as I was," she said, turning back to finish making the salad. "I only saw your father cry two times in his life—the day you were born and the day he told me about the affair."

"But how could he have done that to begin with?" Chance asked, unable to understand how a man could do something like that to the woman he loved.

"Back then, riders didn't fly home after a rodeo," Marlene said, setting the salad on the table. "They had to drive from one to another and that required them to be away from home for weeks at a time if they wanted to make any money at it. Your father got lonely and Ruth was there when I wasn't." She shrugged. "And I suspect alcohol was involved because after that I never saw your father take another drink."

"That's still no excuse for sleeping with another woman," Chance insisted.

"He was a man, Chance." She smiled sadly. "And men make mistakes. Some of the mistakes they make can be easily fixed, while others can't." Laying her hand on his arm, she looked him square in the eyes. "I know how much you worshipped your father and how disappointed in him you were when you learned that he wasn't perfect. But remember this, son. He had already ended the affair and I would have never known what he'd done if he hadn't told me right after it happened."

"Why did he tell you?" Chance frowned. "He could have kept his mouth shut and you wouldn't have had to suffer through all the emotional upset."

Marlene nodded. "That's true. But your father was an honorable man and if he hadn't told me and begged my forgiveness for what he'd done, it would have eaten him alive." She opened the cabinet, then handed him some plates to set the table. "I want you to think about the kind of courage it took for him to make his confession. He stood a very real chance of losing everything he loved. But he couldn't live with that kind of secret between us." She reached up to cup his cheek with her hand. "Don't let his one error in judgment distort your memories of him. He was every bit the good, upstanding man you've always thought him to be."

Chance realized that his mother was talking about more than just his father. In her way, she was telling him not to let his father's one failure affect the choices he made.

As he set the table, then went to tell Fee and Cassie that dinner was ready, he thought about what his mother had said. It was true his father had made a grievous mistake. But the man had been compelled to be truthful and make amends, even though it could have cost him his marriage. That did take a hell of a lot of courage. But it had also been the right thing to do.

Standing at the doorway of the great room, Chance watched Fee and his niece still playing with the dolls. Had he been too harsh in judging his father for simply being human? Had he used Charles Lassiter's transgression as an excuse to avoid falling in love?

When Fee looked up and smiled at him, his heart stalled. He could see his future in her eyes and he had a feeling that if he didn't find the answers to his questions, and damned quick, he could very well end up regretting it for the rest of his life.

When they returned to ranch headquarters after having dinner with Marlene and Cassie, Fee knew she should spend the rest of the evening going over her notes and at least make another attempt to get Chance's agreement to be the family spokesman. It had been days since she'd thought about improving the Lassiter family image, the job promotion she wanted or her life back in L.A.

Why didn't that bother her more? Just a couple of weeks ago, all she could think about was becoming the vice president in charge of public relations. Now, it didn't seem to matter as much as it once had.

"Thanks for being so patient with Cassie," Chance said as they entered the house. "I can't believe all the questions a five-year-old can come up with."

"I didn't mind at all. I enjoyed being with her." Smiling, Fee forgot all about her concerns regarding her lack of interest in the job promotion as she thought about his niece and the fun she'd had playing fashion show with the child. "Cassie's a bright, inquisitive little girl with a very active imagination."

He laughed as they walked down the dark hall toward the stairs. "That's a nice way of saying she's a handful."

"I could say the same thing about her uncle," Fee teased as they went upstairs.

When they reached his room, Chance led her inside, closed the door behind them and immediately took her into his arms. His wicked grin promised a night filled with passionate lovemaking, and the thought of what she knew they would be sharing caused her pulse to beat double time.

"I'll show you just how much of a handful I can be," he whispered. His warm breath feathering over her ear caused excitement and anticipation to course through her.

Lowering his head, he kissed her, and his desperation was thrilling. He wanted her as badly as she wanted him. His need fueled the answering desire deep inside her and stars danced behind her closed eyelids from its intensity.

"I thought I would go out of my mind this evening, watching you and not being able to touch you," he said as he nipped and kissed his way from her lips to the hollow below her ear. "All I could think about was getting you home."

"What did you intend to do when we got here?" she asked, feeling as if there wasn't nearly enough oxygen in the room.

"This for starters," he answered, tugging her mint-green tank top from the waistband of her jeans. Pulling it over her head, he tossed it aside, unhooked her bra and whisked it away. When he cupped her breasts with his hands, he kissed one taut nipple. "And this," he added, paying the same attention to the other tight peak.

Fee impatiently grasped the lapels of his chambray shirt, releasing all of the snaps with one quick jerk. Shoving the fabric from his shoulders, she placed her palms on his warm bare flesh.

"I love your body," she said, mapping the ridges and valleys of his chest and abdomen with her fingertips. "It's absolutely beautiful."

His hands stilled for a moment as he took a deep breath. "Guys have too many angles and hard edges to be beautiful," he said, his voice deep with passion. "But a woman's body is softer and has gentle curves that drive a man crazy with wanting," he added, gliding his hands down her sides to her hips. "That's true beauty, sweetheart."

As he unfastened her jeans, his heated gaze held hers and the promise in his dark green eyes stole her breath. He didn't need just any woman. He needed her. The knowledge sent a wave of heat washing over her and unable to remain passive, she unbuckled his belt and released the button at the top of his jeans.

Neither spoke as they stripped each other of their clothing. Words were unnecessary. They both wanted the same thing—to lose themselves in the pleasure of being joined together as one.

"I need you," Chance said as he kicked the rest of their clothing into a heap on the floor.

"I need you, too," she said, her body aching to be filled by him.

Without another word, Chance lifted her to him and Fee automatically wrapped her legs around his waist. Bracing the back of his shoulders against the wall, he lowered her onto him in one breathtaking movement. Fee's head fell back as she absorbed his body into hers, the feeling so exquisite it left her feeling faint.

He immediately began a rhythmic pace that sent a flash fire of heat flowing through her veins. All too quickly Fee felt herself climbing toward the culmination of their desire and she struggled to prolong the sensations, even as she raced to end them.

Her body suddenly broke free from the tension holding them captive and she gave herself up to the pleasure surging through every cell in her body. She heard Chance groan her name as he thrust deeply into her one last time, then holding her tightly against him, shuddered from the force of his own release.

As they slowly drifted back to reality, Chance suddenly went completely still for a moment before he cursed and set her on her feet. "I'm so sorry, Fee," he said, closing his eyes and shaking his head as if he'd done something he regretted.

"What are you sorry about?" she asked, becoming alarmed by his obvious distress.

When he opened his eyes and looked directly at her, she could see guilt in their emerald depths. "I was so hot and needed you so much, I forgot to use a condom."

Fee's heart came up in her throat and her knees threatened to give out as she made her way over to the side of the bed to sit down. She'd never had to face the possibility of becoming pregnant before. "I can't believe this."

Reaching for the folded comforter at the end of the bed, she wrapped it around herself as she tried to think. The possibility that she would become pregnant from this one time without protection had to be small. She remembered reading somewhere that there was only a 20 to 30 percent chance of success each month when a couple was trying to become pregnant. Surely that percentage went down significantly when a couple only had unprotected sex once. Of course, all of that meant absolutely nothing to the women who became pregnant after just one time in defiance of the statistics.

"Fee, look at me." Chance had put on his boxer briefs and was kneeling in front of her. Taking her hands in his, he shook his head. "I'm sorry, sweetheart. It's my fault and I take full responsibility."

Staring at him, it was her turn to shake her head. "I can't let you take all the blame. I didn't remember, either."

He looked as if he might be calculating the odds. "I doubt that you'll become pregnant from this one time." He took a deep breath and gently squeezed her hands in a comforting gesture. "But if you do, I swear I'll be at your side every step of the way."

"I'm sure the probability is small," she said, distracted.

What was wrong with her? Shouldn't she have a stronger reaction to the circumstances? Or was she simply in a state of shock?

Before she could sort out her feelings, Chance lifted her to the middle of the mattress, removed his boxer briefs, then stretched out beside her. Covering them both with the comforter, he pulled her into his arms and cradled her to his chest.

Kissing the top of her head, he ran his hands along her back in a soothing manner. "Fee, could I ask you something?"

Still trying to sort out her reaction to the turn of events, she simply nodded.

"I know our deal was for you to stay two weeks," he said slowly. "But I'd like for you to stay here with me until you go back to L.A. Maybe by that time we'll know for sure if you're pregnant."

"Okay," she said slowly.

She really didn't want to go back to the rental house Lassiter Media had provided for her. For one thing, she would miss Chance terribly. And for another, being alone while she waited to see if their carelessness had produced an unexpected pregnancy wasn't something she wanted to do.

"There's something else I'd like to know," he said, clearing his throat.

"What's that?" she asked.

"Would it be so bad if you did have my baby?" he asked quietly.

Leaning her head back, she searched his handsome features as she tried to formulate an answer. How could she explain what she didn't understand? Part of the reason she was struggling with the situation was the fact that she wasn't nearly as upset at the thought of being pregnant as she would have been just a couple of weeks ago.

"I'd rather not be pregnant," she finally said, trying to be as honest as possible. "But if I am, the answer is no. I wouldn't mind at all for you to be the baby's father."

Sitting on a bale of hay outside the feed room in the barn, Chance propped his forearms on his knees and stared down at the toes of his boots. He should be shot, propped up and shot again. Not even when he was a teenager with more hormones than good sense had he forgotten to use protection. It was something his uncle J.D. had stressed from the time he'd had "the talk" with Chance and his two cousins when they entered puberty until they all went off to college.

What had been different about last night? Why had he lost control with Fee when he'd never done that with any other woman?

If anything, he should have been more careful with her than he'd ever been. He'd fought against it—had even tried to deny it was happening—but she meant more to him than life itself.

His heart stalled and he felt as if he'd taken a sucker punch to the gut. It was the last thing he'd thought would happen, but he'd fallen in love with her.

As he tried to catch his breath, he realized he'd been a damned fool. Although Chance had no intention of telling Gus, the old cuss had been right. Fee wasn't a woman a man had a little fun with and then moved on from. She was the type of woman a man wanted in his life, his bed and his heart. Forever.

So what was he going to do about it? What could he do about it?

He knew she had feelings for him. Otherwise, she wouldn't have slept with him, nor would she have agreed to extend her stay with him. But she had made it clear she wasn't looking to get involved in anything long-term. Of course, if it turned out she was pregnant, he couldn't think of anything more long-term than raising a kid together. But that didn't mean she would marry him, nor would he expect her to. As far as he was concerned, marriage should be based on love, not because a baby was on the way.

"Whoa!" he said aloud. Was he really thinking about marriage?

As he turned the notion over in his mind, he wasn't certain that was something he wanted to do. He still hadn't completely forgiven his father's infidelity, even though his mother obviously had. If a man like Charles Lassiter could stray, what guarantees did Chance have that he wouldn't?

When he looked up to see Fee walking down the barn aisle toward him, Chance knew he had his answer. He would rather die than do anything to hurt her. If temptation presented itself, he had no doubt that he could walk away from it without so much as a backward glance.

But he wasn't going to spring the idea on her just yet. He needed to think things through and do a little planning.

"Did you finish helping Gus get everything cleared up from supper?" he asked, unable to stop grinning.

"He's already retired to his room for the Rockies game," she said, nodding. She tilted her head to one side. "You look happy. What happened?"

When she reached him, he patted his thigh. "Have a seat, sweetheart. I have something I want to ask you."

She gave him a suspicious glance, then sat down on his leg and put her arms across his shoulders. "What?"

"I intended to ask you the other day when I picked up the tickets, but forgot about it once we had lunch with Dylan and Jenna at Lassiter Grill." He gave her a quick kiss. "Would you like to go to the finals rodeo events at Cheyenne Frontier Days with me?"

"That sounds like a lot of fun," she said, smiling. "I've never been to a rodeo before."

Her delighted expression caused a warmth to spread from his chest throughout his body. She looked happy and he knew there wasn't anything he wouldn't do to please her.

Taking a deep breath, he placed his index finger under her chin to tilt it up until their gazes met. "We both know I'm not overly comfortable being in the public eye," he said, choosing his words carefully. "It's just not my thing. I'm happy staying right here on the ranch, doing what I do best—taking care of livestock and arguing with Gus. But I've been thinking if you really want me to be the Lassiter family spokesman, I'll do it as long as we limit it to just a few pictures and a video or two."

Her excitement was palpable. "Really? You're going to do my campaign?"

"Yeah, I'll do it," he said, loving the way she threw her arms around his neck. When she gave him a kiss that left them both gasping for breath, he decided right then and there, he'd climb a barbed wire fence buck naked if that's what she wanted.

"Let's go back to the house," she said, standing up to take him by the hand.

"Why?" He hooked his thumb toward the horse stalls. "I thought you might like to go for a ride."

She gave him that look again—the one all women used when they thought men were being overly obtuse. "You're about to get lucky and you're going to stand here and tell me you want to go for a horseback ride?"

"No, ma'am."

"I didn't think so," she said, laughing as he hustled her toward the house.

Eight

A week after Chance told her he would be her spokesman in the ad campaign, Fee should have been elated. She had scheduled the first video shoot for the following week, had the first of the on-air spots reserved for the commercials and was well on her way to becoming the vice president of public relations at Lassiter Media. So why wasn't she thrilled?

She knew exactly why. Her time in Wyoming was drawing to a close and when the videographer left to go back to L.A. to edit the footage, she would be returning with him. A lump clogged her throat and for the first time in her life, Fee understood a little more about the choices her mother had made all those years ago. It was going to be the hardest thing she'd ever had to do to walk away from this man.

Blinking back tears, she decided not to think about it now. She would face that day at the end of next week. For now she was with him and she wasn't going to waste a single minute of what little time they had left together.

Seated in the huge covered grandstand with him, she turned her attention to the men on horseback as they roped calves. As soon as the animal had been stopped at the end of the rope, the cowboy would jump from his horse, tie three of the calf's legs together with lightning-fast speed, then wait to see if it stayed bound for a specified length of time. It was interesting to see how fast the cowboys accomplished the task and the level of skill they all possessed. She admired them all for their ability, but quickly decided if she had to do the task it might never get done.

Glancing over at Chance, she smiled. He had been wonderful telling her about the rich history of Frontier Days, explaining the way cowboys were awarded prize money and points toward qualifying for the National Finals Rodeo at the end of the year and patiently answering her questions about the different events. Fee found all of it fascinating and enjoyed every minute of what she'd seen thus far.

"What's next?" she asked, looking forward to more excitement.

"Saddle bronc riding," he answered, nodding toward horses that were being loaded into the bucking chutes. "This is one of the events my dad competed in."

"From what Gus told me, your father was very

successful at this and another event," she said while they waited for the action to begin.

Chance nodded. "He competed in the bareback riding as well as the saddle bronc riding." He smiled proudly. "Dad was world champion in both events several times before he retired."

"How old was he when he decided to quit?" she asked.

"He was thirty-six," Chance answered, staring at the media pit across the arena in front of the other grandstand.

She looked to see what he was so interested in all of a sudden. "Is something wrong?"

"No, I was just checking to see who was operating the cameras this year," he said, shrugging. "Lassiter Media donates the use of some of their audio and video equipment every year and I was just checking to see if any of the Lassiter technicians I'm acquainted with are helping out."

"I didn't realize those big screens belonged to Lassiter," she said, noticing for the first time the huge screens mounted on top of long trailers pulled by semis.

He nodded as he checked his watch. "We've donated the use of equipment for the rodeo as long as I can remember."

"I'll have to keep that in mind," she said thoughtfully. Even though she doubted she would need the information for publicity, it was nice to have it just in case.

When Chance checked his watch again, she frowned. "Do you have somewhere you need to be?"

"Not really." He grinned. "I was just thinking it's about time to get something else to eat."

"Where on earth do you put all that food?" she asked. They had stopped by the chuck wagon cook-off when they first arrived at the rodeo grounds and enjoyed heaping plates full of some of the delicious fare once fed to the men on cattle drives in the old West. "I'm positively stuffed."

"I've used a lot of extra calories the past few weeks," he said, his grin suggestive. "Especially at night."

"Forget I mentioned it," she said, laughing.

When one of the chutes opened and a cowboy on a horse burst into the arena, Fee turned her attention to the action in front of her. At times, all four of the horse's hooves were off the ground as the animal appeared to do aerial acrobatics in its effort to dislodge the rider. Well before the eight-second buzzer went off, the unfortunate cowboy landed on the ground in an undignified heap while the horse continued to buck its way around the arena.

"He doesn't get any points for that, right?" she turned to Chance and asked.

"Nope. He won't get a score, money or points," he answered, checking his watch before he rose to his feet. "While you watch the rest of the saddle bronc riding, I think I'm going to see about getting some food on a stick and maybe a basket of nachos. Do you want me to bring you a corn dog or something else?"

"No, thank you. But before you go, maybe you could explain something to me."

He nodded. "Sure, what do you want to know?"

"Why do men and children like their food on a stick?" she asked.

Laughing, he leaned down to kiss her cheek. "Sweetheart, fair food always comes on a stick and just tastes better that way. Same goes for food at a rodeo."

"I'll take your word for it," she said, unable to believe how many different foods had been put on sticks, dipped in batter and deep-fried at today's event. At one concession stand she'd even seen a sign for fried ice cream—on a stick, of course.

"Will you be all right?" he asked. "I'll only be a couple of minutes."

Smiling, she nodded. "I'll be right here when you get back."

As she turned her attention to the action in front of her, she marveled at the fact that most of the cowboys were able to stay in the saddle for even eight seconds. If she tried to ride a horse like that, she'd be lying on the ground after the first jump.

When the announcer informed the crowd that the saddle bronc event was over and the bareback riding was about to begin, she sat back in her seat to wait for Chance. What could be keeping him so long? Surely he wasn't visiting every concession stand in his quest for food on a stick.

"Dear, I'm sorry to bother you, but would you

mind letting me out?" an elderly woman asked, pointing to the aisle a few seats away.

"Not at all," Fee said, smiling. She stood up to allow the woman to pass in front of her.

"Thank you, dear." The older woman sighed. "My grandson decided he needs another soft drink."

Fee started to tell the woman it was no trouble at all when she heard her name over the public address system. She hadn't been paying attention as she spoke with the woman but now, when she looked up, she was riveted. There was Chance on the huge video screen across the arena, and he was asking, "...Will you marry me?"

She hadn't heard the beginning of his message, but she didn't need to. Chance was asking her to marry him? Why would he do that? And why did he have to do it in such a public way?

He'd made it perfectly clear weeks ago that he didn't want a permanent relationship. She knew he was fond of her and that he desired her, but he hadn't once told her that he loved her.

It suddenly dawned on her that the man who said he wasn't looking for anything permanent had only made the gesture because he thought she might be pregnant. She couldn't think of anything more humiliating than to be blindsided with a marriage proposal in a huge crowd when all Chance was trying to do was assuage his conscience.

The camera scanned the crowd, then zeroed in on her, and she gasped when she saw herself on the giant screens on either side of the grandstand. Her larger-than-life image wore the legendary deer-in-the-headlights expression and when the crowd started chanting "say yes," panic set in. She had to get out of there. She needed time to think and a rodeo arena filled with thousands of strangers wasn't the place to do it.

She felt as if she couldn't breathe as she quickly descended the steps of the grandstand. She'd fallen in love with Chance in spite of all her best efforts not to and if he loved her, his grand gesture would have been sweet and she would have seriously considered agreeing to be his wife. But she refused to marry a man who didn't return her love and only offered because there might be an unexpected pregnancy.

Fee wasn't her mother. She wasn't about to enter into a marriage because a man felt obligated to offer or because he was trying to rectify a mistake. She wanted him to love her as much as she loved him.

Digging through her purse, she managed to retrieve her cell phone. Her hands shook so badly she almost dropped it as she called and arranged for a cab to meet her on the street outside the rodeo grounds. As she made her way to the exit, she decided not to go back to the house Lassiter Media had rented. It was the first place Chance would look for her and at the moment, he was the last person she wanted to see.

No, she was going to the airport to buy a ticket on the first available commuter plane to Denver. From there she could take a flight back to L.A. It was where she could think and where she had the best chance of forgetting the cowboy who had broken her heart.

When Chance saw the look on Fee's face and watched her take off as if the hounds of hell were chasing her, his heart sank. She wasn't just getting away from the cameras. She was making a run for it. He didn't know exactly where she would go, but he knew as surely as he knew his own name that he wouldn't find her anywhere on the rodeo grounds.

Checking with the security office to make sure he was right about her leaving, one of the older guards recognized him as a Lassiter and, taking pity on Chance, showed him the surveillance tape of Fee hurrying through the east exit. Thanking the man, Chance went straight to his truck and climbed in. He felt like a damned fool. He'd gone against every one of his reservations about being the center of attention, told her he loved her and asked her to marry him in front of thousands of people, and she had thrown his proposal back in his face.

He'd told her how uncomfortable he was in front of a camera. Didn't she realize what his gesture meant—that he loved her and was sincere when he asked her to marry him?

He drove straight to the rental house. He knew better than to think Fee would go back to the ranch. The Big Blue was the last place she'd go because she knew he would be there.

The fact that she obviously didn't want to be

around him made Chance feel as if someone had reached in and ripped his heart from his chest. But as he navigated downtown Cheyenne and finally turned onto the street where the rental was located, he shook his head. What had he expected? Beyond great sex, they had very little in common. She was a city girl who had made it crystal clear she was more interested in climbing the corporate ladder than having a man in her life. And he was a country boy who would rather spend his nights gazing at billions of stars in the western sky than watch the moon rise over a skyscraper in L.A.

Parking his truck, he got out and walked up to knock on the door. The rental car was still in the driveway, but when Fee didn't answer, he walked back to the truck and sat there for several long minutes. She was either inside and just not answering the door or she was elsewhere. His money was on the latter.

As he started the truck and drove away, he decided that either way it didn't matter. She'd let him know in no uncertain terms what was important to her. And he wasn't it.

"Momma, Uncle Chance said Fee flew the car a few days ago," Cassie said, skipping ahead of Chance as they entered Hannah and Logan's house after their weekly trip for ice cream.

When his sister and brother-in-law walked into the foyer, Hannah gave Chance a questioning look. "Coop," he corrected. "Fee flew the coop."

"Yeah, that." Cassie frowned. "I was going to tell her today that I decided to call her Aunt Fee."

"Maybe you can tell her another time, sweetie," Hannah said, her gaze never leaving Chance's. "Logan?"

With his usual perceptiveness, Logan Whittaker nodded. "Cassie, why don't you and I go watch that new video cartoon Grandma Marlene got for you?" Logan suggested. "I think your mom wants to talk to your uncle Chance." He nodded at Chance as he led Cassie toward the media room. "My wife is amazing. If anyone can help you see the error of your ways, she can."

Chance frowned. "The error of *my* ways?"

Logan shrugged. "Take my word for it, ninety-nine percent of the time it's a man's fault."

"Let's go into the kitchen and I'll make us a cup of coffee," Hannah said, leading the way down the hall. "You look terrible. You haven't been sleeping well, have you?"

"Not really." When they entered the room, Chance sat down at the table in the breakfast nook while his sister started the coffeemaker. "There's really nothing to figure out, Hannah. I'm here and Fee isn't. End of story."

He appreciated his sister's concern, but he'd lain awake in his big empty bed for the past three nights, wondering how he could have been so wrong about Fee. He'd been sure she had started to care for him the way he cared for her. Obviously, he'd been wrong. Otherwise she wouldn't have left him standing at the rodeo looking like the biggest fool on the whole damned planet.

"Why don't you tell me what happened and let me decide if there's a way you might be able to turn this around?" She sat his coffee in front of him, then took a seat on the opposite side of the table. "Marlene said Gus told her you went to Frontier Days with Fee and came home without her."

Chance groaned. He should have known Gus would send out an alert to all interested parties. "Do you three have some kind of hotline to keep tabs on me now?"

"No, but that's a thought," Hannah shot back. "Now are you going to tell me what happened or am I going to have to get Logan in here to put his cross-examination skills to good use."

"You had to go and marry a lawyer, didn't you?" Chance said, stalling.

He had always been of the opinion that the more you picked at a wound the longer it took to heal. But as much as he wanted the aching in his chest where his heart used to be to end, he suspected the pain of Fee's rejection would be with him for the rest of his life.

"Yes, but don't hold Logan being a lawyer against him," Hannah said, grinning. "I had my doubts at first, but all in all he's turned out to be a pretty good guy. Now, tell me what happened."

Knowing his sister wasn't going to give up until she got to the bottom of what took place between him and Fee, Chance shrugged. "I asked Fee to marry me and she took off."

Hannah shook her head. "I know that. If Marlene hadn't told me, I would have read about it in the newspaper." She gave him a sympathetic smile. "It's not every day a Lassiter proposes and gets turned down in front of a crowd of people."

"Yeah, it wasn't pretty," he said, still disgusted with himself.

"So start over. You've left out some important details. What happened between our wedding reception and you asking Fee to marry you?"

When he told her about the deal he had come up with for Fee to stay with him on the Big Blue, he had to admit it didn't sound all that good. "Looking back, it wasn't one of my better ideas."

"You think?" Hannah asked sarcastically. "If you weren't my brother I'd swear you were a snake in blue jeans and boots. It sounds like you were planning her seduction more than you were trying to talk her out of making you the Lassiter family spokesman."

"I realize that now." He ran his hand over his face as he tried to wipe away some of the regret. "But at the time, all I wanted was to keep things light. I wasn't looking for anything permanent and she made it clear she wasn't, either. I figured we could have a little harmless fun together and when the time came, I'd go my way and she'd go hers."

Hannah shook her head. "It backfired on you, didn't it? You fell in love."

Chance nodded and took a sip of the coffee Hannah had placed in front of him. He really didn't want it, but he didn't want to hurt her feelings. He'd caused enough of those lately. He didn't want to add more. For the past couple of months, his mother had been upset because he made it clear he resented her not telling him about Hannah years ago, Cassie was upset that Fee had left and he'd obviously upset Fee when he asked her to marry him. Hell, he was beginning to think he couldn't win with females.

"So you fell in love, but Fee didn't?" Hannah prodded when he remained silent.

"To tell you the truth, I'm not sure," he admitted. "I thought she felt the same as I do. At least, she acted like she cared for me. But that obviously isn't the case."

"Trying to get something out of you is like trying to pull teeth." His sister sighed. "What gave you the idea she loves you? And did you actually tell her you love her?"

"I didn't tell her until just before I proposed," he answered, staring at his coffee cup.

"Well, what did she say?" He could tell Hannah was getting frustrated, but he didn't particularly care to share the most embarrassing moment of his entire life.

"I don't know what she said because we weren't together," he admitted.

"Okay, you're going to have to tell me how that works," Hannah said, looking confused a moment before her eyes narrowed. "Don't tell me you called her or sent her a text."

"No. I'm not that boneheaded." As he explained about telling Fee he loved her and proposing on the big screen at Frontier Days, he realized he should have told her sooner and in a more private way. "That might not have been the right timing." He'd figured that out on the lonely drive back to the Big Blue that same day.

"Oh, my God, Chance," Hannah gasped. "You seriously didn't do that, did you? I assumed you had told her you love her previously. I wasn't aware that was the first time."

Nodding, he finished off his coffee. "Once again, not one of my better ideas."

"Having a man tell her for the first time that he loves her is a very tender moment for a woman," Hannah said slowly, as if choosing her words carefully. "She doesn't necessarily want an audience of thousands to intrude on that. Especially when they're chanting *say yes* to a marriage proposal she didn't expect."

"Yeah, I got that when she took off," he said, nodding. He shook his head as he decided that he might as well tell Hannah the entire story. "There's something else."

His sister nodded. "I thought there might be. What else happened?"

"Nothing. At least not yet." He took a deep breath. "It's probably remote, but there is the possibility that Fee might be pregnant."

"That's the real problem right there," Hannah said, her tone adamant. "I don't think it's that Fee doesn't love you, Chance."

"Yeah, what's not to love?" he asked sarcastically. "I'm the guy who can't even propose to a woman without screwing it up."

"Don't be so hard on yourself," she said, placing her hand on his. "It really was a sweet gesture and if circumstances were different, everything might have worked out the way you intended. But I wouldn't be the least bit surprised if Fee thinks you proposed only because of the possible pregnancy."

The thought had crossed his mind, but that wasn't the case at all. Unfortunately, Fee didn't know that. "To tell you the truth, that had nothing to do with my decision to propose."

He had realized he loved her the night they had dinner at his mother's. But Fee didn't know that and if there was even the slightest possibility he could convince her, they might still have a chance.

When he remained silent, Hannah's eyes sparkled with excitement. "You're going to Los Angeles, aren't you?"

"I'm thinking about it," he said, feeling more hopeful than he had in the past three days.

Hannah got up and rounded the table to give him a hug. "I realize we haven't known about each other for more than a couple of months, but you're my brother and I want you to be happy. Take that leap of faith, Chance. You'll never know if you don't."

"Thanks for the advice, Hannah." He hugged her

back. "At first I had a real hard time with the fact that our dad had an affair with your mother. But if he hadn't, I wouldn't have you and Cassie in my life. And that's something I wouldn't trade for anything."

"I know what you mean," she said, nodding. "It took me a while to forgive my mother for not letting me know that I had a family who wanted me in their life. But letting go of the past has a way of making way for the future." Hannah gave him a pointed look. "And speaking of the future, you have something you need to do."

"Yeah, I guess I do," he said slowly.

Hannah took the cordless phone from its charger on the wall and handed it to him. "Now, call the Lassiter hangar and make arrangements for the corporate jet to take you to Los Angeles. You have some serious groveling to do." Laughing, she added, "And if you can refrain from making any more grand declarations in front of thousands of people, you might get another chance with Fee."

Chance shook his head. "You just had to bring that up, didn't you?"

"Of course." She smiled. "I've heard sisters are supposed to do that."

"Do what?" he asked, frowning.

She laughed as he dialed the phone. "Remind their brothers when they've been real boneheads."

Nine

"Hi, Becca," Fee said as she closed the door behind her friend. "Thanks for coming over."

"What's up, Fee?" Her friend looked concerned. "You sounded stressed when you called. Is everything all right?"

Fee shook her head. "Not really."

"Since you asked me to come over instead of meeting you somewhere for lunch, I assume you need a shoulder," Becca said, sitting in the chair flanking Fee's couch.

The director of the Lassiter Charitable Foundation, Becca Stevens had asked for Fee's help with publicity on several different occasions for the charity events put on by the Lassiters. Over the years, they had become good friends and frequently shared the highs and lows of their careers—and of their personal lives from time to time.

"Actually, I was going to tell you that there's a very good possibility I'll be leaving Lassiter Media within the next few weeks," Fee said, curling up in one corner of the couch.

"Why?" Clearly shocked, Becca sat forward in the chair. "I thought you love your job."

"I do," Fee admitted. "But after my trip to Wyoming, I think it's time for me to move on."

"What happened in Wyoming?" Becca's eyes narrowed suddenly. "You met a man, didn't you?"

"Yes." Fee shrugged one shoulder. "But I broke the rules."

Her friend looked confused. "What rules are you talking about?"

"Mine," Fee answered. "I got close to someone… and…it's just time for a change." She didn't want to go into details because it was simply too painful to explain.

Sitting back in her chair, Becca shook her head. "But you're in line for vice president of public relations—a position that I know you wanted."

"With my work experience, I don't think I'll have a problem finding another position elsewhere," Fee said, knowing she didn't sound at all enthusiastic about it. She loved working for Lassiter Media and would have continued to work there indefinitely if she hadn't met a ruggedly handsome cowboy who stole her heart.

"Before we talk about where you'll look for another job, tell me about the man you got close to," Becca said gently. When Fee didn't say anything, Becca's eyes grew wide and Fee knew her friend had figured it out. "You got involved with one of the Lassiters."

Tears filled her eyes as Fee nodded. "He's J.D.'s nephew."

"So he doesn't work for Lassiter Media?" Becca asked. When Fee shook her head, she continued, "Then I don't see the problem." She frowned. "Actually, even if he did work for Lassiter there shouldn't be an issue. As far as I know there isn't any kind of company policy on dating another employee."

"It's…complicated," Fee said, sniffing back her tears.

Becca seemed to consider her answer. "I take it that things didn't work out between you?"

"No." Fee closed her eyes for a moment in an effort to regain her composure. "I know it wouldn't happen often, but I don't want to risk running into him at one of the corporate functions or one of your fund-raisers. And I've handed over the Lassiter family PR campaign to someone else for the same reason."

"I can understand that." Becca smiled sadly. "But I'm really going to miss working with you on the publicity for the foundation."

Fee dabbed at her eyes with a tissue. It was completely out of character for her, but for the past few days, everything made her cry.

"Enough about me and my problems," she said,

trying to lighten the mood. "Tell me what's been going on with you for the past month."

"Aside from the fact that donations for the foundation are way down and it's Jack Reed's fault, not a lot," Becca answered.

"He's a corporate raider," Fee commented. "Don't tell me he's started setting his sights on raiding charity foundations now."

"Not exactly," Becca said, her pretty face reflecting her anger. "He's been buying up blocks of Lassiter Media shares in an attempt at a hostile takeover. In light of the way he chops up companies and sells them off piece by piece, our contributors have backed off and haven't been nearly as generous with their donations. Some of the recipients of our funding are shying away from the association with Lassiter Media, too, especially with what's going on with Angelica. She seems to be in cahoots with Jack and that makes everyone nervous. I'm just glad her father isn't alive to see the way she's acting. I don't think he would be overly pleased."

"That's terrible," Fee said, upset by the news. "The Lassiter Charitable Foundation does so much good for so many people. How bad is it?"

"If something doesn't change—and soon—I'm going to have to start making cuts." Becca shook her head. "But I'm not going down without a fight. I'm going to pay Mr. Reed a visit and try to make him see reason."

"I hope you're successful," Fee said, meaning it.

"I've heard he's quite ruthless and doesn't care about anything that doesn't serve his own interests."

Becca took a deep breath. "He hasn't met me. I can be just as cutthroat as the next person when it's something I've worked hard to build and truly believe in."

"Something tells me Mr. Jack Reed has met his match," Fee said, managing a smile.

When Becca checked her watch, she rose to her feet. "I hate to run, but I need to get some things together for that meeting."

Fee rose to give her a hug. "Thanks for stopping by. Good luck and please let me know how it goes. I know if anyone can make Jack Reed see reason, you'll be the one to do it."

"And good luck to you, Fee," Becca said, hugging her back. "I wish you would change your mind, even if you aren't going to do the campaign or get the vice president job. I'm going to miss you terribly."

"We'll still be able to get together for lunch or dinner," Fee offered. "I'll let you know when I get another job."

Opening the door to see her friend out, Fee's breath lodged in her throat and she felt the blood drain from her face. Chance was coming up the walk. Dressed in a white Western-cut shirt, jeans, boots and his ever-present wide-brimmed black hat, he looked more handsome than any man had a right to look.

"Who is that?" Becca asked, sounding impressed.

When Fee remained silent, understanding dawned

on Becca's face. "That's him, isn't it?" She glanced from Fee to Chance and back again. "No wonder you broke your rule. He's gorgeous." Giving Fee another quick hug, Becca whispered, "Good luck working this out with him, too."

Watching Chance tip his hat as Becca passed him on the sidewalk, Fee felt tears threaten. How could she simultaneously be so happy to see him and feel as if her heart was breaking all over again?

"Hi, Fee," he said when he reached her door.

"What are you doing here, Chance?" she managed, thankful that her voice didn't sound as shaky as she felt.

"We need to talk."

"I don't think that would be a good idea," she said, her heart pounding hard against her ribs. Why couldn't he leave her alone to salvage what was left of her heart?

"I do," he said calmly. "Now are you going to ask me in or are we going to discuss this right here on your doorstep?"

Before she had a chance to answer, he placed his hands on her shoulders, guided her back into her condo and shut the door behind them. Her skin tingled from the warmth of his hands even through her clothing and she walked over to put the coffee table between them. If she didn't, she couldn't be sure she wouldn't turn to him and make a complete fool of herself by throwing herself into his arms.

"Why are you here?" she asked again.

"I'm here for your answer," he said simply.

"I thought you would figure out what my answer was when I left Cheyenne," she said, feeling tears fill her eyes.

"Oh, I figured it out right about the time I watched you run down the steps of the grandstand. It was kind of hard to miss on a JumboTron. But I want you to tell me face-to-face," he insisted, taking a step toward her. "You're going to have to look me in the eyes and tell me that you don't love me and don't want to be my wife."

She held out her hand to stop him. "Chance, please don't do this. Please don't…make me…say it."

He held up a DVD case she hadn't noticed before. "Maybe we should go back and replay my proposal so you can see the look in my eyes when you ran away. Then you can give me your answer."

"Why are you doing this?" she asked brokenly. "You don't love *me*. You only asked me to marry you because you think I might be pregnant."

"That's where you're wrong, sweetheart. I told you I love you before I asked you to marry me."

Her knees felt as if they had turned to rubber and she lowered herself onto the couch before they gave way. "No, you didn't. I would have remembered it if you had."

"I wondered if you might have missed that. That's why I brought this along—to prove it." He went to her television and put the disk in the DVD player, switching both machines on.

An image of Chance standing next to one of the rodeo announcers appeared on the screen. The man was saying that someone had a very special message for one of the ladies in the crowd. She watched Chance take a deep breath before he smiled and looked directly into the camera. "I love you, Felicity Sinclair. Will you marry me?"

Fee gasped as she remembered how she'd been distracted by the elderly woman trying to get past her in the grandstand. "I didn't hear you say you love me." She stared down at her tightly clasped hands in her lap. "All I heard was your proposal."

"Believe me, sweetheart, there's no way in hell I would have been on camera with all those people watching if I didn't love you," he stated.

As she thought about the sincerity in his eyes, as well as the number of times he'd told her he wasn't comfortable being the center of attention, she realized what he said must be true. He did love her. "I'm sorry, Chance," she said, wiping a tear from her cheek. "I panicked."

Chance walked over, squatted down in front of her and lifted her chin with his finger until their gazes met. "Just for the record, I'll admit that I'm a pretty traditional kind of guy. But I don't happen to believe that a man and woman should get married just because a baby is on the way."

"You don't?" she asked, loving the feel of his touch, even if it was just his finger on her chin.

He shook his head. "I believe two people should be in love and want to spend the rest of their lives together before they take that step."

"You want to spend the rest of your life with me?"

she asked, feeling hope begin to rise within her, even though the thought of marriage scared her as little else could.

"I do," he said firmly. "I never expected to find a woman I couldn't live without. A woman who invaded my dreams and made me burn for her by simply walking into the room. Then I saw you at Hannah and Logan's wedding and all that changed. I want to spend the rest of my life with you, Fee. I want to make love to you every night and wake up each morning with you in my arms. Is that what you want, too?"

She caught her lower lip between her teeth to keep it from trembling. "I'm…afraid, Chance."

Moving to sit beside her on the couch, he pulled her onto his lap and cradled her to him. "What are you afraid of, Fee?"

The gentle tone of his deep voice and the tender way he held her to him were so tempting. Did she dare trust that his love for her was as strong as hers was for him? Did she have the courage to reach for what she never thought she would ever have?

"I need to tell you why I'm so career driven and why the thought of being in love scares me to death," she said, wanting him to understand part of the reason she'd panicked.

"You can tell me anything," he said, kissing her temple. "There's nothing you can say that will ever stop me from loving you."

"When my mother met my father, she was a successful financial adviser in a prestigious firm in downtown L.A.," she explained. "She immediately fell in love with him and in no time was pregnant with me."

"They got married?" Chance guessed.

"Yes, but I have a feeling it would have never happened if my mother hadn't been pregnant." Fee shook her head. "From what my grandmother told me, my father wasn't the kind of man who stayed in one place for long and he eventually got tired of having a wife and baby in tow. When he decided to leave, he didn't even say goodbye. He just walked out and left us in a second-rate motel somewhere in eastern Arizona with no money and no way to get back to California."

"How did you get back home?" he asked, tightening his arms around her in a comforting gesture.

"Nana sent my mother enough money to pay for a train ticket and the outstanding motel bill." Sighing, she finished, "My mother never got over him, nor did she ever resume her career."

"I'm sorry, sweetheart," he said, gently stroking her hair. "Did he divorce her?"

"A few years after we went back to L.A., she received a set of divorce papers in the mail with instructions to sign them and return them to an attorney in Las Vegas." Fee shrugged. "She voluntarily gave up everything for him and would have followed him to the ends of the earth if that was where he wanted to go. And he couldn't even be bothered to come back and tell her it was over." She shook her head. "Even though they divorced, she held out hope that he would come back one day. She died ten years ago, still waiting for that to happen."

"And you've been afraid all these years that if you fell in love you would turn out like her?" Chance guessed, his voice filled with understanding.

"I know it sounds foolish, but I didn't want to be dependent on a man for my happiness, nor was I willing to give up my only means of support," she answered, nodding. "I didn't want to be like my mother."

"That's something you never have to worry about, Fee," Chance said, capturing her gaze with his. "I would never ask you to give up anything for me or change anything about yourself. I love you for who you are—the intelligent, independent, beautiful woman that took my breath away the moment I laid eyes on her."

Staring into his brilliant green eyes, she knew that she never really had a choice in the matter. She loved this man with all of her heart and soul and had from the moment their eyes met at his sister's wedding.

"I love you, Chance Lassiter," she whispered. Tears flowed down her cheeks as she released the last traces of her fear and embraced the only man she would ever love.

"I love you, too, Fee," he said, crushing her to him. "But I still need an answer, sweetheart."

A joy she'd never known before filled her entire being. "If you'll ask the question again, I'll be more than happy to give you an answer."

Setting her on the couch, he got down on one knee

in front of her. His smile was filled with more love than she ever dreamed of. "Felicity Sinclair, will you do me the honor of becoming my wife?"

Another wave of tears spilled down her cheeks as she nodded and threw her arms around his shoulders. "Yes, yes, yes."

He took her into his arms then and gave her a kiss that left them both gasping for air. "About your career," he said, holding her close. "Do you want me to move to L.A. or would you like to live on the Big Blue ranch and telecommute?"

"Chance, I would never ask you to leave the Big Blue," she said, shaking her head. "That ranch is your life."

He shook his head. "Nope. You are." Touching her cheek, he added, "I love the Big Blue ranch, but I love you more. If living in L.A. is what you want, I'll adjust. My home is wherever you are, Fee."

"I don't want you to give up being a cowboy— my cowboy," she said, kissing him. "I'll move to the ranch and telecommute if that can be arranged." She paused. "If I even have a job with Lassiter."

"Why do you think you wouldn't?" he asked, frowning.

"I handed the Lassiter campaign over to one of my colleagues and told Evan McCain that I might be looking for employment elsewhere," she said hesitantly. "I even mailed the keys to the rental house and the car to the Lassiter Media office in Cheyenne, instead of returning them myself."

"That's not going to happen. You're not going to

lose your job," he said, shaking his head. "I won't be the spokesman unless you're in charge of the campaign."

"But it's all set up with another PR executive," she argued. "They probably won't let me take it back."

"Don't be so sure. I think we can make that happen, as well as setting it up for you to telecommute," he said, laughing. "You're forgetting that your future husband has a little bit of pull with your bosses."

"I suppose you do, don't you, Mr. Lassiter?" she said, laughing with him. "It will make it easier to do the family-image campaign if I'm on the job site." She paused. "You are still going to be my spokesman, aren't you?"

"I'm anything you want me to be, Fee," he promised. "Name it and I'll do it, sweetheart." His expression turned serious. "Now that we have that settled, I have one more question for you."

"What's that?" she asked.

"Don't take this wrong… It really doesn't matter, but I was just wondering… Do you know if you're pregnant?" he asked cautiously.

"I'm not sure," she said honestly. "I haven't taken a pregnancy test."

He nodded. "If you're not pregnant now, you will be eventually."

"You think so?" she asked, grinning.

"Sure thing, sweetheart. The man you're going to marry has been in a perpetual state of arousal since he met you." Chance gave her a sensual grin that sent heat flowing through her veins. "Just say the word and I'll be more than happy to give you all the babies you want."

"Did you hear what I said?" she asked, unable to stop smiling.

Clearly confused, he frowned. "You said you're not sure—that you hadn't taken a test."

Nodding, she kissed him soundly. "The key words in that are *not sure,* cowboy."

As understanding dawned, his grin got wider. "Do you know something I don't?"

"I'm almost a week late," she said, nodding. "Since I'm as regular as clockwork, I would say there's the possibility that the first of all those babies you promised me is on the way."

He wrapped her in a bear hug. "I guess we beat the odds, sweetheart."

"It appears that the remote possibility wasn't so remote after all," she said, hugging him back.

"God, I love you," he said, kissing her cheeks, her forehead and the tip of her nose.

"And I love you, cowboy. With all my heart."

* * * * *

DYNASTIES: THE LASSITERS
Don't miss a single story!

THE BLACK SHEEP'S INHERITANCE
by Maureen Child
FROM SINGLE MOM TO SECRET HEIRESS
by Kristi Gold
EXPECTING THE CEO'S CHILD
by Yvonne Lindsay
LURED BY THE RICH RANCHER
by Kathie DeNosky
TAMING THE TAKEOVER TYCOON
by Robyn Grady
REUNITED WITH THE LASSITER BRIDE
by Barbara Dunlop

COMING NEXT MONTH FROM

HARLEQUIN
Desire

Available August 5, 2014

#2317 THE FIANCÉE CAPER
by Maureen Child
When ex-cop Marie blackmails reformed jewel thief Gianni Coretti into helping her, she expects the sexy Italian to cooperate—not to suggest they go undercover together as bride and groom!

#2318 TAMING THE TAKEOVER TYCOON
Dynasties: The Lassiters • by Robyn Grady
Can good girl Becca Stevens, head of the Lassiters' charitable foundation, keep corporate raider Jack Reed from destroying the family's empire—and win his heart in the bargain?

#2319 THE NANNY PROPOSITION
Billionaires and Babies • by Rachel Bailey
New mom and princess-on-the-run Jenna Peters hides out as a nanny, only to fall for single dad Liam. But will he trust in the passion they've found when her true identity is revealed?

#2320 REDEEMING THE CEO COWBOY
The Slades of Sunset Ranch • by Charlene Sands
Busy raising her infant niece, Susanna is strictly off-limits when her former flame Casey comes back to town. But this rodeo star turned CEO knows no limits...especially when it comes to one very irresistible woman.

#2321 MATCHED TO A PRINCE
Happily Ever After, Inc. • by Kat Cantrell
When a matchmaker pairs Prince Alain with his ex, the scandalous commoner Juliet, he refuses to forgive and forget...and then they're stranded on a deserted island together and old sparks reignite!

#2322 A BRIDE'S TANGLED VOWS
by Dani Wade
Forced to marry for the family business, Aiden Blackstone is surprised by his attraction to his bride. But when someone sabotages his inheritance, can he trust the woman he's let into his bed—and his heart?

HDCNM0714

REQUEST YOUR FREE BOOKS!
2 FREE NOVELS PLUS 2 FREE GIFTS!

HARLEQUIN®

Desire

ALWAYS POWERFUL, PASSIONATE AND PROVOCATIVE

YES! Please send me 2 FREE Harlequin Desire® novels and my 2 FREE gifts (gifts are worth about $10). After receiving them, if I don't wish to receive any more books, I can return the shipping statement marked "cancel." If I don't cancel, I will receive 6 brand-new novels every month and be billed just $4.55 per book in the U.S. or $4.99 per book in Canada. That's a savings of at least 13% off the cover price! It's quite a bargain! Shipping and handling is just 50¢ per book in the U.S. and 75¢ per book in Canada.* I understand that accepting the 2 free books and gifts places me under no obligation to buy anything. I can always return a shipment and cancel at any time. Even if I never buy another book, the two free books and gifts are mine to keep forever.

225/326 HDN F4ZC

Name	(PLEASE PRINT)
Address	Apt. #
City	State/Prov.	Zip/Postal Code

Signature (if under 18, a parent or guardian must sign)

Mail to the **Harlequin® Reader Service:**
IN U.S.A.: P.O. Box 1867, Buffalo, NY 14240-1867
IN CANADA: P.O. Box 609, Fort Erie, Ontario L2A 5X3

Want to try two free books from another line?
Call 1-800-873-8635 or visit www.ReaderService.com.

* Terms and prices subject to change without notice. Prices do not include applicable taxes. Sales tax applicable in N.Y. Canadian residents will be charged applicable taxes. Offer not valid in Quebec. This offer is limited to one order per household. Not valid for current subscribers to Harlequin Desire books. All orders subject to credit approval. Credit or debit balances in a customer's account(s) may be offset by any other outstanding balance owed by or to the customer. Please allow 4 to 6 weeks for delivery. Offer available while quantities last.

Your Privacy—The Harlequin® Reader Service is committed to protecting your privacy. Our Privacy Policy is available online at www.ReaderService.com or upon request from the Harlequin Reader Service.

We make a portion of our mailing list available to reputable third parties that offer products we believe may interest you. If you prefer that we not exchange your name with third parties, or if you wish to clarify or modify your communication preferences, please visit us at www.ReaderService.com/consumerschoice or write to us at Harlequin Reader Service Preference Service, P.O. Box 9062, Buffalo, NY 14269. Include your complete name and address.

HD13R

SPECIAL EXCERPT FROM

HARLEQUIN®

Desire

Read on for a sneak peek at **Robyn Grady**'s
TAMING THE TAKEOVER TYCOON,
the fifth novel in Harlequin® Desire's
DYNASTIES: THE LASSITERS *series.*
The Lassiter legacy is up for grabs, and this means war....

The Robin Hoods of this world were Becca's heroes. As she watched Jack Reed strike a noble pose, then draw back and release an arrow that hit his target dead center, the irony wasn't lost on her.

Jack Reed was no Robin Hood.

Looking *GQ* hot in jeans and a white button-down, Reed lowered the bow and focused on his guest. The slant of his mouth was so subtle and self-assured, Becca's palm itched to slap the smirk off his face.

He freed the arrow from the target, then sauntered over the manicured lawn to meet her. Although he was expecting her visit, Becca doubted he would welcome what she had to say.

She introduced herself. "Becca Stevens, director of the Lassiter Charitable Foundation." She nodded at the target. "A perfect bull's-eye. Well done."

"I took up archery in college," he said in a voice so deep and darkly honeyed the tone was almost hypnotic. "How may I help you?"

"I'm here to implore you, in J. D. Lassiter's memory, to show some human decency. Walk away from this."

He laughed, a somehow soothing and yet cynical sound. "You don't beat around the bush, do you, Becca?"

HDEXP0714

No time. "You own a stake in Lassiter Media and rumors are rife. People are bracing for a hostile takeover bid. The charity's donations are down. Regular beneficiaries are actually looking at other options. Want to guess why?"

"I'm sure you'll tell me."

Damn right she would. "The name Jack Reed means trouble. Seriously, how much money does one person need? Is this worth betraying your friend's memory? J.D.'s family?"

"This is not about money. And make no mistake." His uncompromising gaze pierced hers. "I intend to win."

Becca's focus shifted from the steely message in his eyes to the arrow he was holding. Then she thought of this man's lack of empathy—his obsession with personal gain. How could this superb body harbor such a depraved soul? How could Jack Reed live with himself?

Becca took the arrow from his hand, broke the shaft over a knee and, shaking inside, strode away.

Don't miss
TAMING THE TAKEOVER TYCOON by Robyn Grady.

Available August 2014
wherever Harlequin® Desire books and ebooks are sold.